THE
LAUREL

THE LAUREL

LIZ DEJESUS

BYZANTIUM
Sky Press

Byzantium Sky Press
Ellendale, DE 19941

ISBN: 978-1-955872-28-7 (paperback)
ISBN: 978-1-955872-29-4 (ebook)

Library of Congress Control Number: 2025945534

Manufactured and Printed in the United States of America

Interior design by Crystal Heidel, Byzantium Sky Press
Body of Print book is typeset in Sabon LT Pro
Chapter Numbers of Print book are typeset in Roman SD
Cover Photo © Ironika, Shutterstock id #2020464896

THE LAUREL

PROLOGUE

In a dark cave filled with multicolored strings, and golden cords that hummed with power, sat The Moirae—three sisters—daughters of Zeus and the Titaness Themis: Clotho the Spinner, Lachesis the Allotter, and Atropos the Inexorable. Each one with her purpose, each one with a task that must never end.

Clotho, the youngest of the three, must forever spin the thread of life from her distaff onto her spindle. She was called upon at the ninth month of pregnancy when life must come forth. Lachesis, the middle sister, was tasked to take the thread and measure it, for she decided how long a person would live. And Atropos, the eldest of the three, was the cutter of the thread. She chose the way a person was destined to die. Her golden shears were always sharp and ready.

Lachesis watched Clotho out of the corner of her eye and frowned. "What are you doing?" Lachesis kept measuring the cord.

"What I always do. I spin." Clotho's brown eyes never left her task at hand.

"That's not white mortal thread, nor is it the golden thread that belongs to the gods." Lachesis pointed out.

"I know," Clotho replied.

"Then what are you spinning?"

"I spin a tale that will be told long after the three of us are gone. I spin a tale that will teach a lesson to both god and man."

"Who is this . . . person?" Atropos' voice was gravelly and rough, as though she had spent her entire life drinking water filled with broken glass. "How long will she live so that I may know when to cut the cord?" She cut the air with her golden shears, already eager to put them to good use.

"You won't have to." Clotho kept spinning the cord.

"Don't be silly. Of course I'll have to cut it. It is my job, it's what I do," Atropos argued, waving her shears from side to side.

"She will live on forever," Clotho muttered, continuing to spin a dark green cloth.

Her sisters shook their heads, unable to understand their young sister's strange behavior.

"You speak nonsense, Clotho. I will always have a cord to measure just as Atropos will always have something to cut," Lachesis said.

"That's quite all right, sisters, there is no need for you to understand." Clotho smiled an innocent smile as she spun the thread, feeding it into the spinning wheel.

Their cavern looked more and more like an elaborately decorated, multicolored spider web with every passing day. Clotho created a new cord for each child born into the world. It was a cycle. It was the way the world worked: you are born, you live, and then you die.

But not you, sweet one. We have other plans for you. The world will remember your name, Clotho thought, admiring the dark green thread.

CHAPTER 1

His white wavy hair gently grazed his bronze shoulders as Zeus looked up at the sky with storm grey eyes. He had done well to choose the heavens as his domain. The bright blue always soothed him. He loved it up here; it was far away from the noise of humanity, away from the endless praying and muttering that went on in the world of mortal men.

He couldn't help but smile as he heard Hades curse his name. His brother didn't like the kingdom of darkness, but Zeus knew that it suited him well, given his mood swings and ill temper. Zeus was at peace now that he was far away from the bickering gods and their addictions, although . . . he knew he shouldn't talk. He had his addictions, too.

Ones he enjoyed.

Zeus chuckled as he mentally conjured up the nude figures of some of his favorite lovers. No matter how well he hid himself and his affairs, she would find out eventually. *She* always found out. *She* was always watching him. He burst into laughter when he heard her loud, booming footsteps. This was his favorite part of the day.

The large white doors to the chamber he shared with his wife burst open, leaving behind large cracks where the doorknobs struck the wall. A wild-eyed Hera stood in the doorway glaring at him. His wife was the goddess of marriage and married women. If she couldn't keep her husband faithful, then there was very little hope for mortal women to hang on to their respective spouses. She was losing her followers; everyday fewer women fell to their knees in prayer to her. He knew she couldn't have that. She would lose some of her powers if women didn't believe in her. Unbeknownst to Hera, she was slowly turning into the goddess of jealousy and revenge.

"Where are you hiding her?" Hera roared.

Her red hair flew in different directions, glowing brighter the closer she got to her husband. Zeus stared at his wife. She reminded him of the Gorgon Medusa, a maiden Athena had transformed into a hideous creature with snakes for hair after Poseidon raped her in Athena's own temple. There are many who say that her punishment was just, but Zeus did not agree.

He turned his attention back to his bellowing wife. Hera's locks looked as though they were ready to burst into flames. He already could see some tiny sparks erupting from her skull. He tried to maintain a straight face as he looked at her. His grey eyes remained blank. No emotion. He had to ignore her questions if any of the women in his life were ever to survive.

So, he did what came naturally . . . he lied.

"What are you talking about?" Zeus calmly looked at a clay

figurine that was in an arena he had created. It was his mythical stadium, the scenery changing depending on where the person traveled. It was the best way for him to keep up with the mortals he or any of the other gods were fixated upon.

"You know exactly what I'm talking about. That little whore you've been seeing behind my back. You sneak away like a filthy snake when you think I'm not paying attention. When I find her, you'll wish you had never picked me to be your wife."

She transformed into a beautiful white peacock then glared at him with black, beady eyes. Her beautiful, iridescent, white plumage quivered and then, in a puff of white smoke, she vanished. He knew she had gone down to the world of the mortals in search of his new lover.

Zeus ignored his wife's angry rant and stared at the bright blue sky and the clouds lazily floating above him once more. Hera would never find *her*. She would waste her time for several months. His new lover was a young man, a shepherd. He had succumbed to the god easily enough. That was the way it was with mortals. All he had to do was show them a little power, and they bowed down before him. It was starting to get boring. He wanted something a bit more . . . challenging.

Once, when he was younger, he had loved Hera and no one else. But every day he found women and, on occasion, men who filled him with curiosity. Mortals were such amazing creatures. He wanted to touch their skin, know their thoughts, and feel their hearts beating against his chest. He was fascinated with women of all shapes and sizes, each one a different world. He loved discovering the beauty that existed within every one of them. Women were his weakness. He thought of Hera and knew that she had no heart. The only thing she had inside of her was jealousy, bitterness, and rage. It was a rare sight, indeed, whenever she showed sympathy and warmth toward another being.

Zeus frowned when he heard a soft hum. It was gentle, a whisper with the promise of becoming something more. The rise and fall of the tune held his attention for a long time, until his curiosity got the best of him. He parted the clouds beneath his feet and searched the mortal world for the sound. His heart stopped when he found the source of the music.

I have found you little one, he thought with a smile. *Ah . . . I know who you are.*

He gazed at Leto, daughter of the Titans Coeus and Phoebe, as she bathed in the river. His blood ran hot as he watched her. The clear water glistened and shimmered as it ran down her body. A few drops of water clung to her chin and fell to her chest, leaving a small trail down her abdomen, and lingering on the rim of her bellybutton for several moments.

Zeus' heart skipped a beat as the droplet continued its path until it finally fell down to the river, ending its seductive journey. He was envious of the water that touched her skin. Zeus watched with bated breath and hungry eyes. He wanted nothing more than to be the river that cleansed Leto's body. He would take advantage that Hera was away and visit the new object of his lust. He transformed himself into a quail and descended to the mortal world to meet this beautiful daughter of the Titans.

LETO SPENT MOST OF THE morning helping her friends wash clothes. It wasn't something that she needed to do at home. She wasn't allowed to lift a finger, but she enjoyed using her hands from time to time. The feel of the wet fabric, the slap of cloth against the hard rock, and the rhythmic motion of washing all pleased her. She liked having something to do besides learning poems or studying philosophy. Too many questions riddled her mind day in and day out. All she wanted to do was enjoy herself occasionally and lose herself in something other than complicated questions that truly had no answers.

Now that her friends were gone, she was glad to have a moment to herself. She took a moment to listen to the breeze rustling the leaves on the trees and the happy babbling of the river. Then she noticed something out of the corner of her eye. She jumped and gasped when she saw the large quail. She had never seen one quite so big. They were normally small, terrestrial animals that always seemed in a hurry to get somewhere; however, this particular quail sat calmly and watched her.

Leto couldn't understand why she felt the sudden urge to clothe herself. Perhaps it was the way the quail stared at her. She used her dark brown hair to cover her breasts. She had never seen a quail do anything like this. Normally, birds were nervous little creatures, flying away at the first sign of movement. She climbed out of the river, but the bird still didn't move. He remained steadfast to the spot where he stood.

She gathered her clothes and put on her ivory-colored toga. All the while, she remained apprehensive about the quail.

"Hello," the bird spoke in a loud powerful voice.

Leto's eyes widened as a gasp escaped her lips. She covered her mouth with her hands as though trying to take back the sound she'd made. She had often heard tales of the gods changing into different shapes, sometimes taking the form of animals in order to get closer to people who lived in the mortal world, but she never imagined that it would happen to her.

"Follow me," the bird said.

"Why should I follow you?" She remained uneasy.

The quail shrugged. "You'll just have to trust me."

Leto arched an eyebrow. "If I went around trusting every talking animal that came my way, I wouldn't be a very bright girl, now would I? How do I know you're not trying to trick me?"

The creature laughed. "I like you. Now please, do yourself a favor and do as I ask."

She didn't want to anger what could actually be a god. Still unsure of whether or not she should trust the quail, she reluctantly followed the bird until it stopped in front of an oak tree. Leto studied it and saw gold dust covered the tree. She brushed her fingers against the bark and smiled when she saw that the golden powder covered her fingertips.

A bright flash of light blinded her sight temporarily. She covered her face with her hands until the light vanished. When she finally opened her eyes, she saw the bird was gone, and an incredibly tall man now stood in its place.

His chest was wide, abdomen rippling with muscle, skin the color of bronze, and eyes the color of clouds before a rainstorm, lightning flashing every so often through them. His nose was perfectly straight, lips wide and thin, as though ready to flash a grin at a moment's notice. She had never seen a more handsome man.

"Do you know who I am?" His voice was deep, as though it came from another world . . . which it did.

Leto bowed her head. "I do. You are Master of the Heavens, Wielder of Lightning, and God of gods. You are the Great Zeus."

From the smile on his face she could tell that he enjoyed the flattery and the lovely words she used to describe him.

"I am Leto, daughter of Coeus and Phoebe," she said.

"I know who you are. A daughter of nature, a little Demeter, I might say."

"It is true, I do love nature and I am skilled at it, but I dare not compare myself to a great goddess such as Demeter, one who rules over everything that grows," Leto replied, her head still bowed down, unsure if she should look upon the great god's face.

"You also sing beautifully."

"Thank you. I'm happy it pleases you." She bowed her head and did her best to keep herself at a distance. She knew all too well what happened to his lovers.

Zeus took a step toward Leto. She took a step back without meaning to. She tried not to tremble in fear. He frowned at the action, but quickly understood that she was frightened, so he didn't strike her. Instead, he took a moment to study her face, her body, and her skin. He had never seen flesh so pale. She looked as though she did everything to avoid direct sunlight. He also noticed how tiny she was. He towered above her at nearly seven feet tall. She was small enough for him to wrap both of his hands around her waist.

He reached out to her and caressed her cheek. She gasped when an electric spark snap against her flesh, then she burst into a fit of giggles. Her smile made his heart flutter. It was her smile and her laugh that made him fall in love with her. He had never seen such a beautifully lit face in his life. He didn't know it was possible to enjoy the feel of soft, warm skin beneath his fingertips until now.

He then lifted her face using his large index finger. Leto shuddered in fear. She could feel the static and the power he wielded when he touched her.

"Are you frightened of me?"

"I would be a fool if I weren't, Great One," she replied.

"That doesn't answer the question."

"I am afraid of you, but I'm more frightened of your wife and what she'll do if we are discovered," Leto admitted.

"I will not let her harm you." He promised.

"Is that what you told Io before she was turned into a cow? Is that what you said to Callisto before she and her child were turned into bears?"

Zeus laughed. He hadn't expected her to be so outspoken.

Hearing his laughter made some of Leto's fears vanish.

"We have all heard tales of your adventures and the women you have seduced, Mighty Zeus. What will happen to me if I go to bed with you and we are discovered? What will become of me if I become pregnant with your child? Will you protect the baby? What will happen to me if I let myself be seduced by you?"

Zeus grew silent. He hadn't expected her to ask such deep questions. He never expected any of the women he pursued to question his authority. They always bowed to his will and did as he asked.

"I will make you a queen." He promised.

His promises wove into her mind, making her feel as though she were in a dream. She closed her eyes as she imagined herself draped in the most beautiful diamonds in the world. The word queen danced slowly in her mind like a feather forever floating in the sky. Before she knew it, she said yes to everything Zeus promised.

The oak tree vanished and a golden bed appeared in its place. Zeus carefully guided Leto and placed her on the soft mattress. She sighed when she felt the softness of the sheets against her skin.

"Beautiful, absolutely beautiful," he whispered.

He leaned over and kissed her gently on the lips. Leto shuddered as she felt the gentleness of his lips pressed against her own. Her toga seemed to slip off her shoulders as if by magic. The moment she disrobed his throat went dry. He gingerly kissed her bare shoulder and continued slowly, afraid to move too fast for fear that he might scare her away. He would say whatever was necessary in order to keep her at his side. Zeus had never before wanted a woman so desperately.

What is it about her? He wondered.

She took his breath away. He wished he were the wind so he could touch all of her skin at the same time. He was jealous of the bed that held her body, the sheets that caressed her skin, and the air that brushed against her face as though it had a right to. He wanted to be those things.

Unable to resist her any longer, he climbed atop her. Leto dug her nails into his back, wrapping her legs around his hips, kissing his shoulders. Zeus took one of her breasts in his mouth and gently nibbled on her nipple. He delighted in the lust in her eyes and the soft gasps that emitted from her.

"Oh my goodness," she whispered as she felt her orgasm slowly beginning to build. They gazed at each other's flushed faces, Leto's eyes widening when she saw tiny bits of lightning dancing across Zeus' chest. Her hips rose and fell as she tried to match her lover's rhythm, feeling tiny electric shocks strike her body like a miniature thunderstorm.

Heat quickly spread through her body, feeling as though someone had set her blood on fire and had no intention of dousing her with cool water. She gasped and moaned as she arched her back. Zeus groaned as he felt her nails digging into his back, cutting his skin and drawing tiny droplets of blood. Feeling the warmth of her against his body, he quickly climaxed.

Reluctantly, he lay down beside her. Leto was exhausted from the lovemaking, and even though she struggled to stay awake, sleep eventually overtook her. She snuggled close to Zeus and enjoyed the warmth of his body. Zeus brushed a wayward lock of hair away from Leto's forehead and tucked it neatly behind her ear.

I will love you for all time.

CHAPTER 2

Leto and her neighbor Agnes sat in the garden discussing each other's plants and trading secrets. Leto threw her head back and let the sun shine upon her skin. Normally, she didn't expose her skin to the sunlight. She always wore a long sleeve dress, hat, and gloves when she was outside tending to her plants. She didn't want to get sunburned. But today, for some strange reason, she couldn't get enough of the sun. She basked in it and enjoyed the overwhelming positive energy that seemed to flow around and within her. For several weeks she had been sneaking in and out of the forest to visit her new lover. She was enjoying their lovemaking and his attention. It had been many years since Leto had felt such joy.

"My sunflowers aren't doing so well," Agnes said. "Instead of yellow, they're blooming white. I don't know what that means. You don't think it's a bad omen, do you? I don't need any more bad luck."

Leto opened her mouth to speak and felt the sudden urge to vomit. The back of her throat burned with the acidic taste of oncoming bile. She covered her mouth and shook her head in denial. She knew it could only mean one thing. She stood up, ran to the nearest tree, and vomited her breakfast.

"Are you well?" Agnes ran to her friend's side to see what was wrong. She cringed when she saw the mess on the tree.

"I don't know." Leto walked away from the tree and headed toward the marble bench in her garden.

"You've been seeing someone, haven't you? Well don't just sit there, tell me who he is." Agnes eagerly waited to hear the latest bit of gossip. Her neighbor clapped her hands with excitement.

Leto wiped her mouth with the back of her hand and spit on the ground, trying to get the rest of the bile out of her mouth before she answered her friend's question.

"Zeus," she whispered.

Agnes' skin became white as a sheet. "You can't be serious."

Leto gave her a threatening look. "Do you think I would lie about such a thing?"

"No, no of course not. Forgive me. I was just . . . it's incredible."

"Fool that I am," Leto muttered under her breath. "I should've stayed away and risked getting struck by lightning instead of suffering my ill fate."

"What are you going to do?"

"I will go find him and see if he can help me."

"Do you really think he will?" Agnes asked.

"I won't know unless I ask. Forgive me for cutting your afternoon visit short, but I must leave you."

"I completely understand." Before Agnes could ask Leto another question, her Titan friend and neighbor had vanished.

LETO RAN THROUGH THE forest, her hand protectively over her slightly swollen belly. She stopped to take a moment to breathe. Then she felt the bile running up her throat once more.

"Gods, help me," she whispered before she gathered her long hair with one hand and vomited. She panted and then wiped her mouth clean with her sleeve.

Fool that I am. Now look at the mess I'm in. The gods have damned me. They watch and laugh at my expense while I suffer.

She kept running until she reached the oak tree where she and Zeus had made love. Noticing that it was no longer covered with gold dust, she began to wonder if the encounter with Zeus really had happened or if it had been an illusion.

She knelt beside the tree and called her lover. "Great and Mighty Zeus, I need to speak to you. It is I, Leto, daughter of the Titans Coeus and Phoebe."

Leto waited. Nothing. She tried not to go into hysterics. She could feel her heart hammering against her chest. She gazed at the sky, hoping that he would appear, hoping he heard her call.

Her eyes welled up with tears. She didn't want him to see her crying. She took a deep breath and forced herself to stop, then tried calling him one more time. After what felt like an eternity, Zeus appeared inside a ball of lightning. She squinted as the light died down. She would never get used to his brilliant entrances.

"Hello, my dear," he said with a smile on his face. He looked genuinely happy to see her and eager to give her anything she desired. "What can I do for you?"

Leto's lips quivered like a leaf fighting against the wind. Tears filled her eyes and quickly fell down her cheek.

"My love, please forgive me." She sobbed.

He raced to Leto and held her in his arms.

"Why these tears? What is the matter?" he whispered and kissed her gently on the forehead.

"I'm pregnant," she whispered.

"Pregnant?" he repeated, surprised even though he shouldn't have been. He knew that it would end like this. It always did.

"Please, forgive me. Please, forgive me." She fell to her knees and continued to sob uncontrollably. She was more afraid of what Hera would do to her if she found out about her condition.

"Shh, my dear. Don't cry. I hate to admit that this isn't the first time this has happened to me. We will deal with this quietly. I will do everything in my power to protect you as I promised," Zeus said.

Leto was astonished by how gentle Zeus was being with her. She hadn't expected that from the God of Lightning.

"Where will you hide me?" She spoke as her tears continued to fall.

Zeus thought for a moment. "Go to Xanthos. Once you reach my temple, wait for me to come fetch you. I wish to be present for the birth of my child."

"Why can't you take me there yourself?"

"Because I have hidden you from my wife's sight, and the moment I grab hold of you to take you to Xanthos, you and I will be discovered. The last thing I want is for you to be turned into a large turtle or some other animal that will greatly amuse Hera."

Leto nodded, understanding his reasons. "As you wish." She bowed her head.

He gently lifted her face with his hand. "You bow to no one."

She nodded and blinked, releasing several more tears.

"I will see you soon." He promised.

In a ball of blue-white lightning, he vanished, leaving Leto alone with her thoughts.

Go to Xanthos and wait . . . but for what?

YOUNG DAPHNE SNEAKED A peek at her father, Peneus out of the corner of her eye. She was supposed to stare straight ahead as her father honored her mother by turning her into a river. But curiosity got the better of her and she couldn't help but hide and watch it all unfold. Her father carried his beloved wife in his arms and carefully placed her body beside her favorite stone. Her mother had often sat on that very spot and bathed in the sunlight while she brushed her hair and rubbed small drops of olive oil into her scalp to keep it soft and shiny.

Daphne hated seeing her mother on the ground. So still. So pale. Her eyes closed and her lips missing that joyful smile she always had. It was the stillness that disturbed Daphne the most.

Peneus muttered a few incoherent words and placed his hands over his wife's eyes and stomach. Daphne looked at her sister,

Stilbe and saw that she was looking straight ahead as she was supposed to. Daphne was the only one disobeying their tradition. She took a step backwards when she saw her mother's dead body liquefy before her eyes. Her father had turned her mother into a river. Daphne shrieked when she felt the water touch her toes. She hopped away as fast as she could and climbed a nearby tree.

With the hem of her toga she dried her feet.

"Daphne, do not be frightened," Peneus said, his voice soft and gentle.

"What have you done?" Daphne descended the tree.

"I have given your mother a different form. Now her body will never decay. Instead she will live on in another way. This river will bring much joy to everyone who wishes to visit this place . . . if they are lucky enough to find it that is."

Love makes people do strange things, Daphne thought.

Then she thought about all the peculiar things people did when they were in love. As she watched her mother-turned-river she realized just how truly devastating love was. What it made people do, and how it was almost impossible to let that person go. She didn't want anyone to love her like that. She wanted to be free.

I will never fall in love. I will never allow anyone to have that strong of a grip on me. My heart belongs to me.

HERA WATCHED THE MORTALS running around and going about their business. Mortals were a wonderful source of entertainment when the gods were bored. But Hera wasn't watching them for her amusement. She was waiting to see which one bore an unusual glow. She was looking for her. The one Zeus had slept with two months ago. She hadn't caught them in the act, but she could tell when he had been with her because Zeus looked too happy, far too pleased with himself.

"I'll find her. And when I do . . . she will pay. I will make her suffer for making a mockery out of me and my marriage," Hera said.

She heard a mortal woman muttering and swearing underneath her breath. Hera focused her attention on her voice and willed herself to appear beside her without being seen. She studied the woman closely; she was at least forty years old and not aging well. Her black hair was peppered with grey and she had deep wrinkles in the corners of her brown eyes. Upon closer inspection, Hera noticed that Agnes was barren. But that was easily repairable.

What are you mumbling about, little Agnes?

"Leto thinks she's better than everyone else," Agnes whispered as she swept the dusty floor, "simply because she caught the attention of one of the gods at Mount Olympus. Well, I'll show her. One of these days she won't be so lucky."

Who? Do you know who? Which god? Which one? Tell me. Give me a name, any name.

It was as though Agnes heard Hera's thoughts—moments later Agnes said, "The God of Gods himself. Never would I have thought she had it in her to catch that one."

Agnes stopped sweeping, placed her hand on her hip, and shook her head in disbelief, still unable to come to grips with the things that were happening so close to her home.

With that, Hera made her appearance known to the begrudged woman. Agnes' jaw dropped, but she quickly recovered and fell to her knees. She bowed and showed her respect to the goddess of marriage.

"So tell me, what else do you know about my husband's affair?"

"What will you do to me if I tell you?" Agnes pleaded.

Hera grabbed Agnes by the jaw and, squeezing it tightly, hissed, "What do you think I will do if you don't?" Hera released her grip on Agnes and took a step back.

For a moment, Agnes said nothing. She knew of Hera's wrath and what happened to those who instigated it. She thought of how lonely she had been these past few years, the fact that her husband had left her because she was barren. He had deserted her as soon as he found out that he was not the reason they had been childless for so many years. He had an affair with another woman from their village and had brought home his newborn child to prove it to her. His green eyes had been cold and accusing, as if saying it was all her fault. That was the last she had seen of him. Her yearning made her brave now. "I will tell you everything you need to know if you promise to help me have a child."

Hera looked into Agnes' hopeful brown eyes. She took a step toward Agnes and kissed her. She pushed a tiny speck of light through her lips and forced it to travel to Agnes' womb, repairing the damage that had been there since the day Agnes had been born, planting a seed that would spring forth life, a being so perfect that all would love her child the moment they set eyes on his face.

"You will give birth to a son in nine months. He will be strong.

He will be a good son to you. Now tell me everything you know about my husband," Hera said.

Agnes, overcome with joy, told the goddess everything she knew about Zeus' affair with the beautiful Titaness.

HERA SAT ON HER BLUE velvet throne. She threw her legs on the armrest and waited for her husband to come home. She had a soft smile on her lips the entire time she stared at the door. Even the servants were wary of her when she looked so pleased with herself. An hour later, Zeus appeared at the entrance of his home.

"Where were you?" Hera made sure that her voice was nothing but sweetness and honey.

"It is none of your concern," he snapped, confused with his wife's sudden change of mood. He waved his hand at her as though he were trying to swat an annoying fly away from his presence.

"It is my concern when I have an *unfaithful* husband. I grow tired of having everyone gossip and laugh at my expense." She hissed, slinking out of her throne with the ease and grace of a cat, approaching her husband with lightning speed.

"Believe me, no one is laughing at you." He pressed his face closely against hers. It was something he knew she didn't like.

"Do not mock me, I'm not in the mood." Hera pulled away.

"You are never in the mood for anything."

"Do you think this is funny? Is this some great, elaborate joke to you? Because I am not laughing."

"Trust me, no jokes. No tricks." He promised.

"Would you rather me be a random whore than your wife?"

"Anything would be better than the frigid ice queen that lies next to me at night."

Hera hissed and pulled her hand back, she looked as though she were ready to strike him, but thought better of it.

"You bastard. You think I don't know about Leto? Or that she carries your bastard child? Do you truly believe that I don't know what happens in the mortal world? That I don't know who you're screwing while I sit here alone, unattended, watching you?"

Zeus ground his teeth as lightning danced over his body. "Do not speak her name. Do not ever speak of her. Never utter her name with such spite. Never!" he roared.

Hera froze when she saw his reaction. He was normally very nonchalant about his lovers. He always seemed cool as a cucumber whenever they came up. That he went into a rage over Leto actually frightened Hera more than anything.

"Do you love her?"

He remained silent. He knew better than to answer that question.

"Do you?" Hera's voice softened. The color of her hair turned blood red at the thought of her husband being genuinely in love. She thought of all the things that they had once said to each other—sweet words, promises made when they were young and full of so much love.

Zeus saw the momentary transformation in his wife's demeanor, the look of nostalgia in her eyes, and for the first time in years he ached for her. He, too, remembered the promises he had made. He also realized that he had kept none of them. Hera then remembered all of the lies he had told her throughout the years and the moment was lost forever to them. This wasn't something she had expected.

She asked him the same question once more and again . . . no reply from him. Her blood boiled and her face reddened. She walked away only to grab a marble statue of his head and throw it at him. Her hair blazed like fire once more.

He lifted his hand and lightning shot out from the palm. The marble statue exploded and became a pile of dust on the clean white floor. Zeus strode toward his wife and grabbed her by the throat.

She clawed at his hand with her long, sharp nails. Her blue eyes bulged as her face slowly turned crimson.

"Control yourself, woman," he said.

"I curse her . . ." She croaked. "May she never . . . give birth on mainland."

Zeus growled and threw her halfway across the room. A burst of energy escaped his body and destroyed the room, his body glowing with the sudden release of power. White and electric blue sparks danced all over his body. The white of his eyes glowed bright silver.

"I will take care of you when I return. In the meantime . . . why don't you sit on your *throne*," he commanded.

"No!" she shouted.

Before she could protest, she vanished and reappeared in a dark cave sitting on a golden throne with elaborately designed peacocks. She screamed in horror when she realized where she was. He had placed her on the throne her son, Hephaestus had given her years ago. She wouldn't be able to move unless her deformed son willed it so. How would she convince her blacksmith son to get her out of this throne before Zeus' child was born?

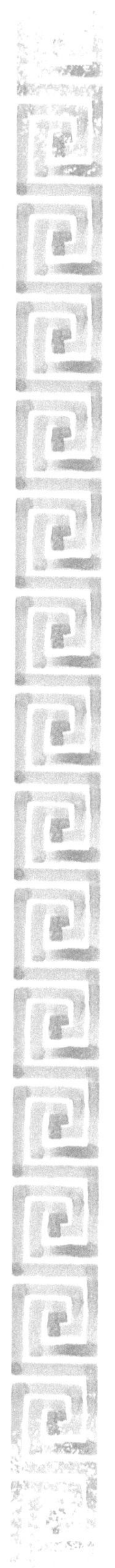

CHAPTER 3

Zeus walked into Hephaestus' workroom where the disfigured god was busy banging away at a large sheet of gold.

"Hello, son," Zeus said.

"I am not your son." Hephaestus reminded him, continuing to beat his hammer on his anvil, creating tiny golden sparks that shot up toward him.

"Nonsense." Zeus gave him a nonchalant grin.

Hephaestus snorted. "If I remember correctly, the last time we spoke was six years ago, and you said 'I am not your father. You were not born of my seed. You are not my son.' Did I forget anything?" He stopped working and arched his eyebrow at Zeus.

"No . . . you did not," he replied.

"What do you want?" Hephaestus knew there was a reason for the visit.

"Your mother is sitting on the throne you made for her when you first visited us at Olympus," he said.

Hephaestus couldn't help but chuckle. He knew the throne of which Zeus was speaking. He had never worked on anything so hard as he had that golden throne. It was perfect in every way imaginable.

"Whatever you do, do not let her off that throne," Zeus warned.

"What will you give me?" Hephaestus wiped the sweat off his forehead. He felt confident in his domain. He stood erect, proud with his hammer firmly in his hand. This was the only place he wasn't afraid of his father or anyone for that matter.

"Anything your heart desires." Zeus' voice was soothing, powerful, seductive. He sounded like a man that was capable of giving you anything . . . and he was.

Hephaestus let the words float around his mind like feathers drifting endlessly through the sky. He thought of how lonely he was in his home. How he longed for a companion, or a child even. He wanted laughter to echo through the walls of his domain. Something besides the constant beating and clinking that surrounded him day in and day out.

"All right," Hephaestus whispered.

"But right now, I have other matters to attend to," Zeus said. "You will get your wish when I return, only remember what I said. Do not let your mother off that throne."

"As you wish." His son bowed his head as his powerful father walked out of his domain.

Hephaestus thought about what he wanted. He was excited at finally being able to serve the Mighty Zeus. His thoughts of reward were interrupted when he heard his name being called out to him, the sound soft in his ear like a lullaby he only heard in his dreams.

"No!" He shook his head. He growled as he hit his forehead with the heel of his hand when he realized who it was. Hera, his mother. "Get out of my head."

"Let me out, and I will give you all the things you wish. What your heart desires," Hera purred.

"No," he shouted, "I cannot trust you. You are a liar."

"So is your father," she said.

"At least he didn't throw me off Olympus the day after I was born," he cried.

Hera let out an exasperated huff of air. "I already apologized for that."

"You took three years to apologize. You can rot on that throne for all I care," he replied.

"I can make you handsome."

Hearing those words caused his heart to jump. Even though he knew that he was not as deformed as his family made him believe, it was still something he was self-conscious about. For a split second he considered Hera's promise. He shook his head. "So can Zeus. Be quiet and stay on your throne."

She laughed in response but didn't say another word for the rest of the day. She had planted the seed of doubt in his mind. All she had to do now was wait.

LETO BORROWED A BLACK HORSE from Agnes. It was a beautiful creature named Cyd. She gently caressed its cheek and whispered softly as she allowed the sweet beast to get used to her presence.

She had never seen such a fine animal. She was eager to mount Cyd and head toward her destination. Leto gently brushed the black horse's mane while she waited for Agnes to come outside and bid her farewell. She couldn't help but notice that her friend had been acting strangely the past few days. Leto didn't know why, but for some reason she felt that she could no longer trust Agnes.

"Where are you going?" Agnes handed the reins to Leto.

"Athens," Leto lied.

"Land of Athena. Why are you going there?" Agnes' brown eyes shimmered with curiosity.

Leto wasn't sure how she felt about her friend asking so many questions. She wanted to keep her pregnancy quiet from all ears until she reached her destination. For a moment, she regretted telling Agnes of her condition. She wished she had lied to her instead of telling her everything. She let out a deep sigh. All she could do now was wait until Zeus told her what to do next or at least gave her a sign, something that would inspire some hope for her future.

"The gods will it. I have to go," she replied.

"I apologize. I can't help being curious about where my horse is going," Agnes said as she gave Cyd a gentle pat on his forehead.

"Don't worry. You'll get your horse back. Thank you for your kindness, Agnes. You are a good friend." Leto embraced Agnes. She couldn't understand why something that had once felt normal and natural was now odd and queer, as though she were embracing a stranger for the very first time. She let go of Agnes, the awkward feeling still lingering in the air. "Well . . . goodbye." Leto grabbed the reins and climbed onto the four-legged beast.

"Goodbye, Leto. Good luck to you in your journey." Agnes smiled.

Once more, Leto couldn't shake the feeling that there was something wrong with her friend. The smile Agnes gave Leto seemed fake, but she didn't have time to ask questions or make accusations. She had to go to Xanthos and wait for Zeus as fast as possible. She rode off into the woods, her belly growing larger with every passing day. She hoped and prayed that she wouldn't have to give birth to her child on the ground.

What are you doing Zeus? What are you doing that keeps you away from me?

HERA SAT TRAPPED ON HER throne, in a room surrounded by gifts that had been tossed aside because they were no longer useful or needed.

She was thinking of multiple ways to keep Leto from giving birth on land. She wanted to drive her toward the rivers or lakes, into the sea so that she may drown along with her bastard child. She thought until she thought a hole into the ground. Then she remembered her pet python, Kiril.

"Come to me, my pet. Precious Kiril. Come to me," she whispered.

After several hours of waiting, a black python softly and slowly slithered its way toward its mistress. Kiril's mauve tongue flicked in and out of its mouth as it drew closer to Hera.

"Hello, my pet," Hera purred.

Kiril lovingly rested its diamond-shaped head on Hera's lap. Hera wished she had been able to move her hands so that she could pet Kiril, but the throne she sat upon limited her mobility. She could only move her neck and her head, only those parts of her that were not touching the throne.

"I am a prisoner here," she whispered. "Unable to move freely. Kiril, my sweet pet, I need you to be my eyes. Find Leto. Chase her. Bite her. Do not let her have a moment to rest until you have driven her to a river, lake, or ocean," she commanded. "Do not rest until she has drowned herself in desperation. I want to see her cold, lifeless body visit Poseidon's kingdom at the bottom of the sea. Do not let her feet touch land." Hot, angry tears escaped Hera's eyes.

Kiril gave her a soft hiss as a reply and slithered away to carry out her command.

"Do not fail me," she muttered, watching the black snake leave the room.

ZEUS WAS IN THE GARDEN OF Hesperides picking an apple for his unborn child. He noticed the Three Graces dancing and singing a few feet away from him. He chuckled as he watched them hold hands and spin around in circles until they fell to the ground from dizziness. A string of giggles escaped their lips as the lime green grass tickled their backs. His willful daughters were kept here because he couldn't bear the thought of a man taking advantage of their kindness, charm, and generosity. They didn't seem to mind taking care of the garden. They had everything they could ever want.

He turned his attention back to his task. He took a long time choosing this fruit. It had to be perfect in every way. He needed to do this properly. He plucked a golden apple from a tree that his mother Gaia had planted especially for occasions such as this. It was also a wedding gift she had given Hera when she had accepted to be Zeus' wife. He thought about that moment. The smile on her face when she had said 'Yes.' How bright and shining it was. How happy she was that day and many days afterwards. He shook his head and tore that image of her out of his mind. She was no longer that bright and shining woman.

He broke off a branch from a silver tree. He wanted to have Hephaestus make a flute out of it. He grinned as he imagined the look on Leto's face at the sight of such lovely gifts.

Then he frowned as he heard a loud hiss coming from the world below.

Why does that sound familiar to me? It's as though it were something that came from a nightmare I had when I was younger. Something is wrong. What did that woman do?

He knew that the throne wouldn't necessarily stop Hera from causing trouble, but at least it would keep her out of the way for a few months while Leto traveled to a safer place.

He closed his eyes and searched for Leto. He found her easily; she was riding a black horse toward Xanthos, just as he had asked her to. Her belly was growing larger.

Where did she find a horse?

He was impressed with her resourcefulness. He didn't know

what it was about Leto that captivated his heart so, but he knew no harm must come to her. He must keep her safe at all costs.

What is it about you, beautiful Leto?

He then searched for his wife, The Ice Queen, as he liked to call her.

"Humph," he snorted when he found that she was where he had left her. She must have sensed him looking at her because she screamed and cursed his name.

I've heard enough of that to last me a lifetime.

He opened his eyes and went back to his task. But no matter what he did to distract himself, he couldn't shake the feeling that something was still strangely amiss.

Hiss.

Leto opened her brown eyes when she heard the sound. The sky was pitch-black. There was nothing above her head except the twinkling, shimmering stars and the waning silver moon. She sat up and looked around. The only thing she could see was the bundle of burnt wood from her fire, half of which had turned into a pile of ashes. Nothing. No movement anywhere save the horse beside her, breathing calmly.

Maybe it's all in my imagination.

She rested her head on the bundle of clothes she had turned into a makeshift pillow and tried to ignore the sound.

Hiss.

She gasped and scrambled to her feet. Cyd, sensing her distress, woke from his peaceful slumber, and was alert within seconds, ready to gallop away.

Something evil comes for me, Leto thought as goose bumps covered her body. She quickly packed her things and mounted the horse. She rode away, deeper into the woods, into the enveloping darkness, without really knowing if she was being paranoid or if there really was some grave danger out in the night.

HEPHAESTUS BEAT HIS HAMMER against a large sheet of copper. He pretended he was beating his hammer against his father's face. He hadn't heard anything from Zeus in weeks, and had the feeling his father wasn't going to keep his word.

"Father," he called to him with his mind. He hoped that Zeus was listening.

"Yes?" Zeus replied within moments.

Hephaestus was a little surprised at how quickly his father answered his call. He regained his composure. "When are you going to return?"

"I don't know," he said.

"Are you going to keep your promise?"

"You know I will keep my word, but I cannot talk about this right now. I have more pressing matters to attend."

"More important than your son?"

"There are lives at stake here. I will not put them at risk because you can't wait until this is finished," Zeus argued.

"But . . ."

"Do not interrupt me with this again," Zeus warned.

Hephaestus felt the connection break. He couldn't help but feel shut out . . . alone. He threw his hammer against the wall and growled in frustration.

If it had been Ares, Hebe, Eris, or Eileithyia, he wouldn't hesitate to give them what they wanted. But me? *I have to constantly wait. I'm always second best. No. Not second. Dead last.*

CHAPTER 4

AN EXHAUSTED LETO COLLAPSED ON TOP OF CYD WHO, BY some miracle, continued to carry the Titaness on his back even though he was panting and foaming at the mouth from fatigue. Her limp arms and legs fell to the side of the four-legged creature. Tears fell freely down her cheek, landing softly on the ground she had been unable to touch for the past two weeks. She had realized quickly that Hera was aware of her condition and was doing everything possible to make her suffer.

"Zeus," she whispered her lover's name as though she were beginning a prayer. She had tried to continue the journey on her own, without having to ask for his help, but now she felt as though she had no choice. "My love . . . help me." Her voice cracked. "Help me. Please."

She could feel her growing body slowly rolling off the horse and knew she was moments away from crashing onto the ground. There would be nothing she could do about it. She braced herself for the impact of the ground only to find that someone was there to catch her. Someone had saved her from falling onto the ground.

"I'm here." Zeus suddenly appeared and caught her in his strong arms. "Don't worry, Leto, I am here."

Her eyes opened wide with surprise. She gasped with relief and couldn't help but break into a fit of sobs when she saw his face. She extended her hand to caress her lover's face only to realize she was in too much pain to do that. She hissed in agony and let her hand fall down limp beside her.

"What happened?" he demanded.

He couldn't believe his eyes as he took in the sight of her. Dark circles marred the perfect pale skin beneath her brown eyes. A dull emptiness replaced the twinkle in them; he couldn't stand to see it. Her skin looked ashen and dirty as though she hadn't bathed in weeks.

"I tried . . ." Her voice sounded hoarse, as though it hadn't been used in months. "I tried not to call you for help." Leto buried her face in his chest and cried.

"Shh, my beautiful, it's all right. Now tell me . . . what happened?"

"A snake chased me. No sleep in weeks."

Zeus knew that his jealous wife had kept her word. He kissed Leto's forehead. He thought about taking her to Xanthos himself and risk Hera seeing them together, but he knew that things would become much worse for Leto if he did that. Even if Hera weren't watching his every move, Xanthos would be the very first place she would search for Leto.

Where can I take you? He wondered as he gazed at his lover's worn out face for an answer. He thought for a few moments until an idea finally came to him.

"Of course," he whispered to himself. "Why didn't I think of that before?"

Delos. It was the only place he knew where no one would be able to find her because the island constantly moved about freely several feet beneath the ocean.

Before Zeus vanished with his precious cargo, he turned his attention to the brave horse that had carried his lover on its back without rest.

"Brave Cyd. You will have your strength replenished, and your offspring will be a gift to my unborn child," he whispered into the creature's ear, "but until then, you will rest here peacefully. I will fetch you when the time is right."

The black horse happily closed its eyes and collapsed on the soft ground.

"Now for you, my dear." He turned his attention back to the woman in his arms. In an instant, he willed them both to Delos. Only Zeus and Poseidon knew the exact location of this floating island. This place would be a haven for Leto. Zeus was the only one to have set foot on this place. The water reached his knees even on the highest ground. With one arm, he cradled Leto close to his body. He then extended his other arm and brought the island up to the surface. An overflowing rush of seawater made way for the new ground that had yet to be touched by the light of the sun. Zeus brought forth flora and fauna on the island so Leto had something to eat and drink when she awoke.

With a single thought he created a small home for Leto close to the beach. It had every comfort he could imagine a woman and child would need. It had thick sturdy walls to protect her from harsh weather. A soft bed, tables, chairs, and a kitchen. Remembering how much she loved to garden, he made certain there was fertile soil around the house so that she could plant seeds and garden if she wished to do so. He walked inside the house and gently placed his lover on the bed. Beside her, he made sure to add a small crib for their unborn child. The only thing missing was a place for him by her side. He knew there wouldn't be a place for him in this sanctuary. All he could do was ensure her safety.

Finally, he placed a protective spell around Delos so that he would be the only one able to find this tropical paradise.

"I will leave you here where you will be safe. I swear it," he whispered into Leto's ear.

He studied the curves of her face, and felt the softness of her skin as he gently touched her with his fingertips. He curled a bit of her long brown hair between his index finger and his thumb. He smiled when he saw the golden glow in her womb. He took a closer look at the child growing within. There was powerful magic growing within her. He frowned when he saw that the light had split into two. He chuckled and then broke into a loud joyful laughter when he saw two children softly suckling on their thumbs, eyes tightly shut. He still couldn't tell if the twins were a pair of boys or a pair of girls. Not that he cared. He was thrilled either way.

You are full of surprises, aren't you? He stared admiringly at his beloved Leto.

ZEUS DECIDED TO GO DOWN to the bottom of the ocean to pay a visit to his brother. He wanted to talk to Poseidon about the floating island. He always took his time whenever he went to his brother's kingdom under the sea. There was so much to see, and so many new creatures to discover. The last time he had been here, he saw a swordfish for the first time. He remembered talking to Poseidon about what it would be like to see a fish that could defend itself, and he was surprised to find that Poseidon had taken that conversation seriously.

No matter how many times he visited the underwater kingdom, he always marveled over the beautiful glowing city. Every tower looked like the sharp point of Poseidon's trident. Large, peach coral reefs decorated the entrance of the palace where Poseidon resided. A school of clown fish sped past him as he floated through the massive whale bone doors. Zeus swam down the hallway until he reached the throne room, and found his brother, Ruler of the Sea, sitting upon his immaculate chair of silver, gold, and pink coral, holding his golden trident in his hand. Poseidon's long, dark turquoise hair floated softly above his shoulders. His blue-green eyes shimmered with curiosity as he watched his younger brother approach him.

"Mighty Zeus, what brings you to my realm?"

"I can't visit my brother to see how he is?"

Poseidon chuckled. He could count on one hand the times that Zeus had visited his kingdom. He knew better than to believe that lie. He asked Zeus once more why he was in his kingdom.

"I have come to speak to you about Delos," Zeus replied.

"What about it?" Poseidon pursed his lips while spinning his trident with a tidal current. It wasn't often that he had something that Zeus wanted. He would be sure to take advantage of this situation.

"What do you want in return for it?"

"Why do you want Delos?"

"A gift for my wife," Zeus lied.

Poseidon roared with laughter. His cackle caused several giant waves throughout the world. He always had to be so careful with sudden outbursts such as this but, for once, he couldn't help himself. He had caught the god of gods in an outright lie.

"Delos? For Hera? I would rather sink the island to the bottom of the sea so that she may never set foot on it," Poseidon said. "Now, let me ask you again, why do you want Delos?"

Zeus had hoped that he could avoid telling Poseidon the truth; he didn't like people knowing about his affairs. He didn't like appearing vulnerable before anyone, especially a mighty ruler like Poseidon. But he thought of Leto and the look on her face when she had seen him.

Zeus took a deep breath and decided to tell the truth.

"Leto. I want the island for Leto." His shoulders fell at the mention of his mistress' name. "She hasn't slept, eaten, or bathed in weeks, and that is the only safe place for her. Hera cursed her. Leto isn't allowed to give birth on the mainland. It is a curse that I cannot remove myself for reasons I will never know. But this is the only way around it. Delos is the only place Hera will not find her. I was able to cast a protective spell around it so that you and I are the only ones who will ever be able to find it. I am trusting you with precious cargo. Now I ask you once more,

Lord Poseidon, Ruler of the Sea, my brother, what do you want in return for Delos?"

The god of the ocean rubbed his chin as he thought about Zeus' request. He was very rarely this adamant about anything. He was certainly stubborn when it came to the women he chased, but not for something like this.

"Have Hephaestus make a new trident for me, and you can have Delos for your mistress," Poseidon finally said.

"Thank you, brother. Your gesture will not be forgotten."

LETO'S EYES FLUTTERED OPEN. Beneath her she felt the softness of a comfortable bed. She sat up and studied her surroundings with a confused look on her face.

How did I get here?

She rubbed her belly as she wandered around the small house. She waddled outside and gasped when she saw the view. She had never seen water that bright and beautiful. The turquoise ocean seemed to go on forever. Then she remembered the *dream* she had.

"He really did come for me." A smile appeared on her lips. This place felt different. It felt untouched by man. Peaceful. She knew that she would be safe here, felt it in every bone and every pore in her body. She took a deep breath and sat on the beach. She grabbed a fistful of sand and watched it slip between her fingers. She was grateful for the silence. She hoped it would last.

"Hephaestus," Hera called out her son's name.

She needed to get out of the wretched throne that entrapped her. She had been sitting for nearly five months, and Leto was still alive. That wouldn't do.

"Leave me alone," Hephaestus shouted from his volcanic domain.

"Son . . . my son . . . if it is beauty, love, and joy that you desire, I will give you Aphrodite," Hera said in a soft, seductive voice.

She grinned when she heard his heart skip a beat.

Ah, I have finally found your weakness, she thought.

"Do I have your word?" He tried to hide the desperation in his voice.

"I will marry her to you myself," she swore. At this point, she was willing to promise him anything so long as it would result in her freedom.

Hephaestus thought long and hard about the offer Hera had just made to him. He didn't want to break the oath he had made to Zeus.

"I will think about it," he replied.

"Hephaestus . . . please," she begged.

"Stay on your throne," he muttered and went back to work.

All day Hephaestus daydreamed of having Aphrodite as his wife. He walked to a nearby mirror and looked at his own reflection, wondering what made him so ugly to the other gods. His hair was the same shade of black as his brother, Ares. His eyes were grey like his father Zeus. He had his mother's thin and wide lips. He was the first to admit that Ares was more pleasing to the eye than he was, but he couldn't understand why he was called deformed because of the scar beneath his ear. A scar that bore testament to the day Hera had dropped him from Mount Olympus.

Such an ugly word, deformed, he thought. *Why should I be associated with such a word? It's not fair. What have I done to deserve such a title?*

"Father," he said.

"Not now Hephaestus," Zeus whispered into his mind.

"What will you give me for keeping mother out of your way?"

"Anything, just not now," he replied.

"Unless you make time, you will give me no choice but to break my vow," he said.

"What do you mean?"

"Mother has promised me Aphrodite as my wife," Hephaestus said.

"Son, you do not want her as your wife, she will only bring you chaos and misery. That woman isn't love and sweetness; don't let her looks fool you into doing something you will regret. Think about it," Zeus warned.

"Enough! I have made up my mind. Hera . . . I release you from your throne," he said.

"NO!" Zeus roared. "What have you done?"

Hera broke into a fit of giggles when she stood from the throne. Her laughter quickly changed into a loud cackle as she stretched her limbs. Twirling on her tiptoes, she let out a sigh of relief.

"Will you keep your promise?" Hephaestus demanded.

"Oh, yes, my son. I have every intention of keeping my promise to you," she replied.

She vanished before Zeus could return to force her to sit upon the throne once more. She searched high and low for Leto, but no matter how hard she looked, she couldn't find the elusive Titaness.

"Curse you!" She hissed when she realized she wouldn't be able to find Leto.

Zeus has hidden his little whore very well.

Hera found a cave close to the Underworld and used that as her hiding place. Zeus very rarely visited Hades' domain. She would be safe here for a while. She paced and thought of ways she could still keep the promise she had made. She wanted Leto to suffer. Hera wanted to hear her squirm and shriek with pain. Then Hera realized that she could use Leto's pregnancy against her. The only reason childbirth wasn't as painful for some women was because Eileithyia was already close by ready to lend a helping hand.

She decided that she would need the assistance of her daughter Eileithyia, the goddess of childbirth. If there was a child being born, Eileithyia was there. The wonderful thing about her was that she could be present in multiple places at once. She never missed a child being brought into the world. Ever . . . at least until now. Hera wasn't sure what the consequence of her daughter's absence would be to other children in the world but she didn't let that concern her.

Hera silently appeared close to Eileithyia. Her daughter was carefully watching over her favorite apprentice, Cassia. Eileithyia tied her long black hair into a loose bun, instructed her student, and kept the woman in labor as comfortable as possible.

"Push, Lydia, push. You can do it," Eileithyia whispered in a calm, soothing voice.

The woman turned bright pink as she held her breath and continued to push her child out of her womb. Eileithyia placed her hand upon Lydia's burning forehead and took the majority of the pain away.

"Oh! I see the head," Cassia exclaimed.

"Shh," Eileithyia gently reprimanded.

Hera couldn't help but marvel over the way her youngest daughter worked, switching places with Cassia, as she brought new life into the world. It almost made her regret what she was about to do. She shook her head.

No . . . I have to do this.

"Push, push, the baby is almost out," Cassia said as she wiped the sweat off Lydia's forehead.

Eileithyia pulled the baby out and let out an excited giggle.

"It's a boy. You have a beautiful baby boy." She held the child up for Lydia to see.

"Oh my goodness," Lydia said between tears.

The goddess of childbirth cut the umbilical cord, cleaned the baby with a pristine white cloth, and handed the child to his mother.

"Thank you," Lydia said.

"You're welcome," she said with a warm smile.

"You can take it from here, Cassia. Something else requires my attention." Eileithyia had sensed her mother's presence the moment she appeared but she wasn't going to allow it to interrupt her work.

"Hello, Mother," she said.

"Hello, Daughter," Hera replied.

"I never knew you to be interested in what I do." Eileithyia wiped her hands clean and arched her eyebrow at her mother. She knew Hera was up to something. She didn't like the way her mother refused to meet her gaze.

"What are you up to?" Eileithyia said.

"I need you to go away for a while. Stop doing what you do," Hera said.

"Are you mad?" Anger emanated from Eileithyia's voice. "I can't stop helping women during childbirth. They could die. Have you no compassion for these mortal women? Have you no respect for my gift and what I give to humanity?"

"I'm sorry, but I need you to do this for me," Hera argued.

"This is about father, isn't it? You always get irrational when he's out cavorting with some mortal woman. Well, I won't do it. I don't want any part of your plans. You cannot just come here and interrupt me whenever it pleases you."

Hera slapped Eileithyia across the face with the back of her hand.

Eileithyia didn't feel a thing, but it was the action in itself that shocked her. She never thought her mother would lay a hand on her in such a way. "Why me? I bring life into this world. I don't want to be a part of whatever hatred runs in your veins.

Go fetch Ares, he's better at destruction. He has your temper. Better yet, why not Eris? She has a penchant for anger and strife." Eileithyia looked at her mother. This was the goddess of marriage? She was supposed to put an end to arguments not cause them. She gazed at her mother and saw nothing familiar inside this angry woman.

"Goddess of marriage indeed," Eileithyia said as she walked away from her mother.

"Don't you dare walk away from me!" Hera roared. She grabbed her daughter's long black hair and pulled her back. "You will be an obedient child, and you will do as I say," she hissed in her ear.

"No, I will not," Eileithyia replied.

Hera let out an ear-piercing shriek, took her daughter to the bottom of the ocean, and tied her to a boulder with a rope Hephaestus had given to Zeus. Only the person that tied the knot could undo it. Eileithyia couldn't believe it. She struggled to free herself, but nothing she did worked. All she could do was call her father.

"Useless bastard! Why can't you follow instructions? Why did you let her go? You don't know what you have done!" Zeus roared, striking Hephaestus across the face with each statement. White lightning rippled across Zeus' body and struck the walls. Hephaestus' workroom smelled sharply metallic and filled with smoke.

"You are the oath breaker. You forgot me," the blacksmith god snapped as he wiped the sweat and blood off his chin.

"You are dead to me," Zeus shouted as he walked out of his son's domain.

"Father," a female voice called softly to his mind.

Zeus frowned. He didn't recognize the voice that called to him. "Who is this?"

"Eileithyia," came the weak reply.

"What's wrong?" Zeus was surprised that she was calling him. He rarely heard from his youngest daughter. She was the only one who didn't cause him grief. She was his perfect little daughter and the only one of his children who looked like him.

Too tired to speak, Eileithyia flashed him an image of where she was trapped. Surprised this time to find out her location, Zeus growled in anger. Then it all made sense. With Eileithyia out of the way, Leto would have all the pain of childbirth. He knew that whatever his wife had done, she would be the only one who could undo it. He made his way back to Mount Olympus. He needed to put an end to this.

CHAPTER 5

All the gods gathered at Mount Olympus, which didn't happen often. If not for some of the male gods having paramours who were pregnant and needing Eileithyia to bring their bastard children safely into the world, it would not have happened this time.

"Where is she?" Poseidon demanded. "My daughter was supposed to be born days ago. Amphitrite has been in labor for two days." He whispered, "She isn't doing well."

Gods weren't used to dealing with pain. They never had to suffer from physical ailments. They never grew old, and they never died. Anytime they had to deal with unpleasant emotions, they did their best to block them out or ignore them altogether. But the way he spoke of his lover let everyone know that he was frightened for her. It was always with Eileithyia's help that mortal women were able to give birth to an immortal child. Without her, there was no hope for them or the children.

"What happened to Eileithyia?"

"Why isn't she doing her task?"

Other gods raised more questions.

"I need everyone to be quiet," Zeus said.

Quickly, silence ensued.

"Hera has tied our youngest daughter to a boulder at the bottom of the sea," he announced.

"What?"

"Outrageous!"

Gasps and outbursts among the crowd of gods surrounded Zeus.

"Only she can undo the binds that hold my daughter prisoner," he added, "so I suggest we all go find Hera."

Within seconds, all the gods vanished.

KIRIL RESTED HIS DIAMOND-shaped head on Hera's lap. His tongue slithered in and out of his mouth slowly, enjoying the way she stroked his body. The python tried to show his mistress that he was sorry he had lost the woman she'd asked him to follow.

"It's all right Kiril. I'm not angry with you," she whispered gently as she continued to stroke his scaly skin.

He hissed a gentle reply.

"You did exactly what I asked of you. It's not your fault Zeus interfered. He always gets in the way of the things that I want to do."

She looked at her surroundings. A dark, damp, and stalactite covered cave wasn't where she wanted to be. It wasn't exactly what she was used to, but it would have to do until Leto was ready to give birth. Hera knew it would only be a matter of weeks before Leto was due to bring her bastard child into the world.

Queen of Gods? What a joke. Look at what I have been reduced to—no wonder everyone laughs at me.

Hera felt her pet python slide off her lap, but before she could protest, she was up in the air. She felt the bones in her neck crunch. Whoever it was had a deadly grip on her throat. She clawed at the air as she tried to free herself.

"Did you really think you could hide from me? That there was a corner of this cursed world that would allow you to be free of me?"

Hera tried to reply, but all that came out was a weak croak.

"Your own daughter? How could you do what you did to your own child?" Zeus appeared, finally letting his presence be known.

Hera's eyes became wild and angry as she looked upon her husband's face. The look she had on her face only made Zeus want to squeeze harder. He wanted to kill her, but instead, he took her back to Mount Olympus where he and the other gods would decide her fate.

"How dare you interfere with the cycle of birth?" Demeter, the goddess of fertility and nature, was outraged when she heard what Hera had done. She was glad none of her children were expecting.

Hera looked away from Demeter's accusing, amber eyes. She didn't need to know how Demeter really felt about her. Everyone knew what had happened to her daughter Persephone and how desperately Demeter was still searching for her.

"Your own child? How could you do such a thing? If only I had my daughter back. I would give anything to see her one last time. How could you?" Demeter suppressed the urge to cry at the thought of Persephone.

Hera glared at all the gods surrounding her. Demeter, naturally, was the first to speak up. It would take a few seconds before Athena chimed in.

"The actions you have taken in the past several months show nothing but how completely irrational you have become," Athena, the goddess of wisdom, said in a deep clear voice, just as Hera had expected.

"Do you have any idea how much pain Amphitrite was in at the birth of my child?" Poseidon roared. He was inches away from striking her against the cheek with the back of his hand, but Zeus acted fast, grabbing Poseidon's wrist.

"She may be a lot of things, brother . . . but she is still my wife," he warned.

"Then contain her." Poseidon spat.

Zeus stood taller and took command of the room. He was their chosen leader whether they liked it or not. What he said was binding.

"Hera, you know why you're here." The god of gods turned his attention to his jealous spouse.

"Naturally," she replied, meeting her husband's stormy gaze.

"Set her free," he commanded.

"And what? Let that whore of yours give birth to your bastard child? I think not," she replied.

Zeus smiled. Hera frowned.

"What are you smiling about?" she snapped.

"There are two *bastards* being born into the world," he said.

"What?"

"Leto is carrying twins."

The earth shook. The seas roared. Plants withered and died. For sixty seconds, the world was thrown into chaos by the sound of Hera's shriek.

LETO PUT HER HANDS protectively around her womb when she felt the ground trembling.

She knows. Gods protect me . . . she knows.

Leto ran to the little house that Zeus had created for her and locked herself inside. Not that it would do her any good. The gods would be able to find her no matter where she went. But being behind closed doors gave her the illusion of safety.

"HOW IS IT POSSIBLE?" Hera shrieked. "Twins? *Twins?*"

"Now until you agree to release Eileithyia, you will have to remain in a very uncomfortable place," Zeus said.

Hera involuntarily shivered. Whatever Zeus had in mind it

would not be pleasant. Zeus grabbed Hera, and along with Poseidon, they tied her arms and legs with golden rope. She squirmed and struggled as she tried to free herself from the ropes, but it was no use . . . these were ropes made by Hephaestus. No one other than the person who tied the knot would be able to undo it. That was the way he liked to make things.

Zeus grabbed Hera and tied her to a cloud. She hung upside down so that she could hear the desperate women clamoring for help, screaming in pain. Hera heard a woman's last breath before finally succumbing to death. For several weeks, this was all she heard.

Finally, unable to take any more, she burst into tears.

I was supposed to protect you all. I was to keep you safe, and I failed. I failed you all because I knew what I was doing and I knew the harm I would cause.

"All right!" she shouted. "I've had enough of this."

"Are you going to release our daughter?"

"Yes, just get me out of here," Hera cried.

Zeus undid the knots and released his wife.

Hera hung her head in shame as she lifted her eyes at her husband. Zeus stared back at her, his eyes cold and angry. She didn't have the energy to glare at him. She went with him to the place Eileithyia was held prisoner and untied her daughter.

EILEITHYIA COLLAPSED ON THE palace floor, needing a moment to take a deep breath. She coughed until all of the water escaped her body and her lungs. She was grateful to her father and the other gods for having helped set her free from her watery prison. She gave her mother a deathly glare as she stood up to her full height.

"I never want to see your face . . . ever again." Eileithyia hissed. She had never known until that moment how much she could hate another being. The fire that now burned in her chest was filled with nothing but hatred for her mother. She turned to her father and whispered, "I have never asked you for anything. Please make certain that she stays away from me."

"As you wish, my daughter," Zeus replied.

She leaned forward and gave her father a gentle kiss on the cheek and a warm embrace. She hardly ever took such liberties with him. "Thank you, Father," she whispered before vanishing to take care of the mortal women in need of her.

The moment Eileithyia reached the mortal world, the cries of desperate women in pain quieted as though a great calming wind caressed their burning bodies.

"You are free to go," Zeus said to Hera.

"What?" Hera was surprised he would let her go after all the trouble she had caused.

"Hera, you have suffered enough embarrassment to last you an eternity," Zeus said. "Please do not make me regret my decision."

"You want me to leave her alone?" Hera mumbled.

"Please," he replied.

"Why should I? Why should I do anything for you when all you've done is humiliate me every chance you get?"

"Because you loved me once. And somewhere deep inside, you

love me still; otherwise, you wouldn't become as jealous as you do every time I stray. I don't humiliate you. I remind you of your place in this world. If anything, you embarrass yourself."

Hera bowed her head in shame. She knew that as long as the world continued to turn, mortals would talk about what she had done to Leto and what she had even done to her own daughter in order to get her revenge.

A GIRL.

Leto was amazed at how painless and effortlessly the child made her way into the world. She barely felt a thing. She was still waiting for the goddess of childbirth to appear. Leto wondered for a moment if she was going to need any assistance from Eileithyia with the other twin. She cut the umbilical cord with a clean, sharp dagger and wrapped her beautiful dark-haired daughter in a white blanket while she waited for the other child to exit her womb. Eventually the pain came, like sharp knives cutting her abdomen. A strangled breath of air escaped her lungs as she tried to make sense of the pain she was feeling. Her legs went numb as though she had never been able to use them before. Leto's body trembled, and she broke into a cold sweat.

It's a boy. I know it. It has to be a boy; otherwise, there wouldn't be this much pain.

"Leto," a voice spoke to her.

She panted, breathing in and out as quickly as she could while doing her best to ignore the voice that spoke to her.

No voices. I don't have time for this right now.

"Leto," the voice spoke more insistently.

"What?" she shouted as she tried to push her son out of the womb.

"I cannot permit him to be born here," the voice replied.

"Who are you?"

"I am Delos. I am the island."

"How is this possible?"

"Zeus brought me to the surface. Before he touched me, I had no life. Once he touched the ground and brought life to this place, he gave me a spirit without realizing it. Your son will be incredibly powerful. His birth will destroy me, and I will be forgotten. I will die. You cannot give birth here."

"Are you the one responsible for all the pain I'm going through?"

"Yes," the island replied.

Leto's vision became blurred from the agony she was in at that moment.

"I promise that once my son is born, you will be given proper homage for allowing my children to be born here," Leto swore.

"People cannot come to an island that is capsized and covered in water," Delos said.

"That won't happen," Leto said as a drop of sweat fell into her left eye. She hissed in pain as she closed her eyes tightly.

"You cannot make such a guarantee, you are not a goddess."

"I am the daughter of Titans!" she shouted as she slammed her fist on the ground, causing the island to shake and quake just as mightily as any god. "My son will be born today."

She then took a deep breath and pushed even though it didn't do anything to help; she pushed with all of her might. Then she felt the island trembling.

"What is happening?"

The island didn't reply. They both remained quiet until the rumbling ceased.

"I am anchored to the bottom of the sea," Delos said. The way the island spoke led Leto to believe that if it had been at all possible, Delos would've smiled with pleasure.

"What does that mean?"

"Your son can be born here," it replied.

"Oh, thank the gods," she said with a sigh of relief.

"Swear on Styx that you will have your son build his temple here on this island," Delos said.

"I swear it. I swear on the River Styx that my son will honor you with a temple." Leto vowed.

Eileithyia appeared moments after Leto made her vow to the island. The goddess of childbirth helped Leto bring her golden son into the world.

"She has given me a son and a daughter," Zeus whispered, holding his blonde son in one hand and his brunette daughter in the other. He looked at his little girl. "You will be named Artemis." Then, to his little boy, he said, "And you will be named Apollo."

Apollo's blonde hair glowed bright yellow. Zeus looked up at the sky, his domain, and glanced at the shimmering sun. *He is as bright as the sun*, Zeus marveled.

Artemis giggled and cooed. She grabbed a fistful of his white hair. He chuckled and then tickled Artemis' cheek until she relinquished her tiny grip. He studied his beautiful little girl and saw that her skin was pale and pearlescent.

And she is as pale as the moon.

He looked at Leto with a newly found love and respect for her. She beamed under his gaze. She was proud she had given him such beautiful children.

"Everyone will remember both their names for all eternity. Mortals will tell stories about them. No one will ever forget our children or how they came to be," Zeus said. "Such tiny fingers," he whispered as Apollo's diminutive hand tried to grab Zeus' giant thumb.

CHAPTER 6

Leto held Apollo and Artemis' hands as she led them up the mountain that would take them to Olympus. She was nervous. It had been years since the last time she had seen Zeus face to face.

Apollo abruptly stopped. "Why are we here?"

Leto sighed. This would be the tenth time in one hour he had asked the same question. No matter how many times he questioned her, she couldn't help but smile at her curious son. All he had to do was grin and all of her frustrations melted away.

"Your father, the Great Zeus wishes to see you both," Leto explained.

"But he sees us no matter where we go," Artemis said.

"That's true, darling, but he wished for me to bring you to Olympus. He wants to see you with his own eyes. He very rarely asks for anything, so I have every intention of indulging him. Now" —Leto stopped walking and looked at her children— "I want both of you to be on your best behavior. Artemis, no climbing trees or chasing after any of the animals in the palace. Apollo . . ." She couldn't think of something he ever did that was actually *bad*. "Don't flirt."

He replied by giving her his best smile. She rolled her eyes and continued with her list of warnings.

"If he offers you gifts, decline them as politely as possible," she said.

"Must we really?" Apollo seemed surprised that his mother would suggest such a thing.

"I don't want you to make a habit of taking advantage of your father's generosity. Now please do as I ask. It's for your own good," Leto said.

Both children sighed in unison. They knew they would have no choice but to do as their mother requested.

"Now if you see any of the other gods with your father, I doubt you will, but just in case, do not speak unless you are spoken to. Gods can be fickle, and they like to pick fights just because they are bored." Leto stopped and looked at the twins. "Are we clear?" She spoke loudly so they both understood the seriousness of her words.

Apollo and Artemis nodded their heads so fast and so hard that Leto thought their heads would roll off their tiny bodies.

"Very well. Let's go," she said.

After hours of walking and climbing up the mountain, they reached the palace. The children gasped upon seeing the tall marble pillars and the beautiful silk curtains that danced gently with the wind. The fabric was a light aqua; Apollo had never before seen such a glorious color in his short life. He reached out, wanting to touch it and feel the softness against his skin, but Leto gently reprimanded him.

"Don't touch, darling," she whispered, and then kissed him on the cheek.

Apollo couldn't believe that he was finally here. He looked around the palace and marveled at the beauty of everything he saw. Even though it was made of clouds, the floor held his weight without any sign of faltering. The pillars were made of white marble. He wandered away from his mother's side and gently touched the sky-blue curtains. He had never touched silk so soft in his life. He had always asked his mother what it was like up on Mount Olympus, but each time she would shake her head sadly and say, "I've never been up to the cloud kingdom."

He saw Leto quicken her steps. He ran to her side before she could notice he had been off to his own devices. He didn't want to get lost in the palace either, so he followed his mother who, though she had never been to Olympus, knew exactly where to go.

Apollo noticed his mother's nervousness at being in Zeus' palace. Apollo and Artemis knew the story of how they came to be. They knew how hard it had been on their mother and all the grief Hera had inflicted upon her. The twins had vowed early on to always protect their mother . . . no matter the cost.

LETO'S DARK BROWN EYES darted nervously from side to side as she took in her surroundings. Zeus had sworn to her that Hera wouldn't be anywhere near the palace for the next couple of days. He had promised her that the children would be safe.

"She's not here, Mother," Apollo said, his clear voice bringing her back to the present.

Leto frowned at her son's choice of words.

"Who's not here?" Leto asked.

"Hera. She's not in the palace."

"How do you know?"

"Because I have already seen today . . . and she's not in it," Apollo said.

"Liar. You didn't see anything." Artemis rolled her ice-blue eyes.

"Don't call him a liar, Artemis. You know I don't like that," Leto gently scolded.

The Titaness relaxed a little. Apollo rarely had visions, but whenever he saw something and spoke of it, she was mindful to listen to his council . . . even though he was only a six-year-old boy.

When they finally reached the throne room, Leto let out a soft gasp when she saw Zeus, the father of her children. He was still as handsome as she remembered him. Still imposing and almighty. Even after all this time he continued to be the love of her life. Zeus sat in the middle of a silver and white velvet throne. White tigers, peacocks, and a large white stag stood close to the god of gods. Her heart fluttered at the sight of her old lover. It had been years since she had felt his warm touch, but she knew that nothing would ever come of their brief tryst. She averted her eyes and reminded herself that she was only here because Zeus wanted to see his children. Even still, her skin cried out for his touch.

Zeus gave his guests a wide and bright smile. He glanced at Leto then refocused his attention elsewhere. He didn't want his eyes to linger and make it obvious how much he missed her. He couldn't believe how kind the years had been to her. She was still as beautiful as the day he had first laid eyes on her. The only thing that gave away that she had aged was a single gray hair in that ocean of dark brown waves on top of her head and a few worried wrinkles on the corners of her eyes. Reluctantly, he turned his attention to the twins.

"Apollo and Artemis, how good it is to see you with my own eyes," he said.

"Hello, Father," they said in unison.

"Hello, Master Zeus. Thank you for kindly inviting us to come visit you," Leto said.

"I'm glad you came. It is good to see you as well, Leto," he said, staring into her dark brown eyes for the first time in several years. "Now" —he stared at his children— "both of you come here. I want to get a closer look at you two."

The children hesitated for a moment. He was still a stranger to them, but they were naturally precocious children. Artemis was the first one to take a step forward. Apollo followed her lead. Zeus studied his daughter, Artemis, and couldn't believe the darkness of her hair.

Black like a crow.

Her skin was pale and her eyes were like the sky on a cloudless day. Zeus gazed into them and found far too much knowledge and wisdom for a young girl to possess. He shook his head, ignored his daughter's attentive stare, and gave her his best grin.

"Now tell me, Artemis, what you would like for your father to give you," he said.

Her eyes grew as large as saucers, and she desperately looked to her mother for assistance. She remembered what Leto had said about gifts, and she didn't want to disobey her mother, but she didn't want to displease her father by rejecting his extremely generous offer.

Leto sighed, giving her a single nod. Artemis beamed as though she were lit from the inside out and turned her attention back to her father, looking more like a six-year-old little girl who had been given permission to ask for whatever her tiny heart desired.

"Now, come and sit here"—Zeus patted his knee— "and tell me what would you like?" Zeus was happy that Leto had changed her mind.

"I want a silver bow and arrow that kills whatever target I have chosen. I want a quiver that never runs out of silver arrows. I want six of the best hound dogs in the world to be with me at all times. I want all the mountains on earth to be my home. I want sea nymphs to be my companions and . . ." Artemis took a breath from her exhaustive list, looked at her mother, and then returned her attention to Zeus.

"And?" Zeus encouraged her.

"I want to be a virgin for all times," she said.

"Really?" Apollo quickly covered his mouth with both of his hands. He wasn't sure if he was allowed to speak, and the last thing he wanted was for his father to be upset with him.

"Is that what you want?" Leto approached Artemis and placed a gentle hand on her daughter's shoulder.

"Yes," Artemis said, looking at that moment much older than six years old. She looked like a crone who had seen far too much of life and was waiting for the Moirae to cut her cord.

"So be it," Zeus said.

He snapped his fingers and everything that Artemis wished for was given to her. She smiled when she saw six puppies. She jumped off her father's lap and went straight toward the bouncing, yelping pups. They climbed all over her and licked her face. She giggled and squealed as she felt their tiny tongues tickling her cheeks.

Leto tried to look like the disapproving mother that knew they were being given far too much, but the smile on her daughter's face was enough to melt anyone's resolve.

"And you son? What would you like?" Zeus turned his attention to the youngest twin.

Apollo slowly and carefully stepped closer toward his powerful father. Zeus studied his son's features. The boy was perfect and, amazingly enough, the exact opposite of his sister. His skin was a light tan as though he spent all of his spare time outside basking under sunlight and his hair sandy blonde. Zeus looked into his son's eyes and marveled over how blue they were, seeing that every single shade of blue that existed in the world could be found in Apollo's eyes.

Intriguing, how these two were even capable of sharing the same womb when they are so different from one another.

Zeus glanced at Leto, and once more felt a surge of pride wash over him for his former lover. She had endured so much to bring such perfect beings into the world. For a moment, he wondered if he would be able to make more children with her. He quickly let the daydream vanish; he had promised himself he would leave Leto alone and allow her to live a peaceful life on Delos. The island was incredibly protective of the Titaness and her children, and few people were allowed to visit the temple that had been built in the center of the isle without Delos' permission.

Zeus turned his attention back to his son, who had already taken a step back when he saw the vacant look on his father's face.

"Are you afraid of me, son?"

"Yes."

"Why?" he whispered.

The little boy walked up to his father and whispered in his ear, "I know of the things you have done."

Zeus flinched and looked as though he had been stung. That was the last thing he had expected to hear from a six-year-old boy.

"Really? And?"

"You are not always a good man," his son replied.

"You are right. But let's not talk about that. Tell me something that you would like for me to give you." Zeus dismissed the seriousness of his son's comments. He would have to remember to ask Leto if Apollo possessed the gift of prophecy.

Apollo wasn't really interested in gifts. He was mostly curious about the type of man his father was. But sensing that Zeus wouldn't take no for an answer, he borrowed some of the things that Artemis said since he couldn't think of anything on his own.

"I would like a bow and arrow made out of gold so that I can hunt with Artemis," Apollo said.

"And?"

"And?" Apollo repeated.

"That's all?"

"Should I ask for more?"

"You can if you like," Zeus said.

Apollo took a few seconds to think about something else that he would want. Something he could use in the future, something that would never ever leave him.

"Knowledge," he blurted.

"Knowledge?" Zeus echoed. He turned his gaze to Leto. "What are you teaching these children? Do you allow them to play? Are they allowed to roll around in the mud and make a mess?"

"Darling, you should know better than to ask me that question. You know how I've been raising them for the past six years," Leto replied. Her gaze lowered as a blush rose to her cheeks. She couldn't use terms of endearment like this on Zeus any longer.

Zeus shook his head and gazed back at Apollo.

"You can have all of the knowledge you want son, but not until you are older. Enjoy being a child while you still can," Zeus replied. He saw the disappointment on his son's face, but he refused to alter his son's mind at such a young age.

"Leto, I would like to speak to you . . . alone," Zeus said.

"As you wish," Leto said.

"WHAT HAVE YOU BEEN telling the children?" Zeus asked.

"Nothing," Leto replied.

"Are you certain? You've told them nothing about us?"

"Of course. Why would I tell them that? I'm not exactly proud of it," she replied.

He muttered a few curse words under his breath; he didn't want to have an argument with Leto. He knew he would lose any battle with her in the room. He sighed, ran his fingers through his hair, and shook his head.

"Why would Artemis want to be a virgin?"

"I suppose she wants to avoid my fate. I don't blame her," she said.

"And Apollo asking for knowledge? He's six years old," he said.

"Dar . . ." she whispered as she inwardly chastised herself. She blushed again with embarrassment; this wasn't what she had come here to do. She didn't want to rekindle their ill-fated romance. She reminded herself that the only reason she was alone with him was to discuss their children. She cleared her throat. "Apollo has the gift of prophecy."

"I guessed as much," Zeus said. He pretended he didn't hear her almost say *darling* again. A rush of warmth had invaded him when she'd said it moments earlier. So much hope in a single word. All he wanted to do was rip off her clothes and take her to his bed. He wanted to kiss her, taste her skin, make love to her. He had never wanted someone so desperately. As he opened his mouth to speak, to change the subject, to talk about whether or not there was a chance for them, Leto spoke first.

"Zeus . . . he can see into the past, present, and future. Sometimes he'll see things from when I was a child. He has seen you being born," she said.

"What?" he whispered.

"He has also seen visions of a girl with dark green hair. He keeps asking about her. He wants to know who she is, but I don't know of whom he speaks. I've never seen or met a creature with green hair. At least not the way he's describing her to me," Leto said.

"A girl?"

"Are you surprised? He is *your* son," Leto deadpanned. "Sometimes, it's sporadic. I don't always know when it happens because he won't talk about it, but some of the things he says are shocking, especially because they're coming from the mouth of a child."

"Do you want me to take it away?"

"Take away his gift of prophecy? You can do that?"

He arched his eyebrow and didn't even answer her question.

"I'm sorry. I'm not used to this." Leto shook her head.

"Well?"

Leto thought for a moment. Prophecy was a part of who Apollo was, whether she liked it or not. "No. He has this gift for a reason. Leave him be."

"If you change your mind, let me know," he said.

"You seem very surprised by the way they've turned out so far. I thought you watched my every move."

"I do watch you every day, but not every hour, every minute or every second. I'll peek in on you and the children in the morning for a few minutes and then at night when you're putting them to bed," Zeus admitted.

"Ahh, now I understand."

"Understand what?"

"Why you wanted to see them face to face," she said.

"I'm not the monster people make me out to be."

"No, you're not a monster. You just love women more than you love your wife," she said.

Zeus let out a sigh as he stared at the beautiful woman standing before him.

"Beautiful Leto." He smiled. He studied her features; her straight nose, small pouted lips that were always a natural pink, and high cheek bones. The whites around her dark brown eyes looked a little pink, as though she had been crying recently. She looked tired, but even that couldn't erase the beauty of the Titaness.

"I know my name," she replied with a coy smile.

"We could always try for another set of twins," Zeus suggested.

Leto giggled and shook her head at the thought of having more of Zeus' children.

"I have a hard enough time dealing with those two on a daily basis. Besides, I don't need another adventure giving birth. Once is enough to last me a lifetime," Leto replied.

"What a shame," he said.

"Why?"

"We make gorgeous children."

"Darling . . . it's just not in us to make anything other than spectacular and beautiful children." Leto smiled, then winked.

Zeus chuckled, remembering full well why he loved Leto so.

"WHAT DO YOU THINK they're talking about?" Artemis paused playing with her new silver bow and arrow and looked at her brother.

"Us," Apollo replied.

"How do you know?" She shot her arrow at an indigo vase. And no matter how many arrows she used, she always had a fresh one. Same thing with the vase, no matter how many times she broke it, it repaired itself.

"I've already seen it."

"Liar," she said.

Apollo sighed and refused to argue with his sister. Sometimes he wondered how they ended up in the same womb. They barely had anything in common.

The doors to the adjacent room opened, and Leto stepped into the hallway with Zeus following close behind her.

"Come, children. It's time to go. Say good-bye to your father," she said.

"Can't we stay a little longer?" Artemis pleaded.

"I wish we could, but the Mighty Zeus has other matters to attend to," Leto explained.

Artemis nodded, looking crestfallen, as she gazed around the incredible palace. But she knew that this was not the time nor place to argue about staying longer. That was not an option.

"Good-bye," the children said in unison.

"Thank you for the gifts." Artemis waved at her father, her new puppies clumsily running after her as they made their way out of the palace.

"Yes, thank you, Father," Apollo said.

"You're welcome, hopefully this won't be the last time you receive gifts from me," he said.

Apollo smiled politely to his father and took his mother's hand. Artemis followed suit and held Leto's other hand. Zeus was saddened to realize there was no place for him to fit in the scene playing out before him.

"Don't worry, we will see each other again." Apollo glanced back at Zeus.

"I'll make sure of it," his father replied.

CHAPTER 7

"Come out, come out wherever you are," Artemis mumbled as she held her silver bow and arrow. Even after twelve years, the silver still gleamed as though her father had given it to her yesterday. Her long fingers expertly held the arrow in place, the bowstring slightly pulled back, ready to release the arrow at a moment's notice.

She played a deadly game of hide-and-seek with Apollo. He had claimed he was a better 'hider' than she.

"If I find you, I'll shoot your leg through and through with my arrow," Artemis had said.

Apollo had smiled.

"Deal." He'd shaken her hand.

Now, Artemis moved through the forest carefully, slowly. She took off her sandals, loving the feel of the moist, soft ground beneath her feet. She made sure to avoid dried leaves and branches, anything that could give her away. Artemis wasn't going to give Apollo any kind of warning. For a moment, she thought she had seen a glint of Apollo's hair, but quickly dismissed it as a bird's feather.

He's making me try too hard. He's my twin. There are a few things that we do have in common whether I like it or not. With that thought in her mind, she closed her eyes and imagined where her brother was hiding. Then, clear as if she were seeing him with her own eyes, she knew. She had to admit it was a good *hiding* place. Apollo was inside a hollow tree. She pulled the bowstring all the way back and released her silver arrow. She heard it whistle and whisper as it flew at rapid speed through the air. The arrow shot right through the dried-up bark.

Apollo shouted as the arrow struck him. Artemis laughed upon hearing a loud thud and ran to the spot. Squirming on the ground was her twin brother with an arrow in his thigh.

"I told you I'd find you." Artemis grinned smugly.

"How did you find me?"

"I closed my eyes and let go of the arrow."

"Liar," he said.

"Call me whatever you like, but I'm not the one on the ground with an arrow stuck in my leg." She placed her dirty bare foot on his bleeding thigh near the wound, and pulled the arrow out.

He growled and tried to keep himself from crying out in pain the ruby-stained arrow emerged from his limb. She carelessly spun the arrow between her calloused fingers then parted her lips ready to insult his hiding skills a little more when she saw the deep frown on his face. Something was wrong. Her body felt cold, as though someone had dumped icy water on her.

"What is it?"

"Mother," he whispered.

She heard it moments later—their mother sobbing and crying. The twins felt as though someone had stabbed them in the chest with every sob that escaped her lips. Their quarrel quickly forgotten, they raced to reach Leto.

The forest became a blur of dark browns and greens as they sped to their home. Apollo didn't break a sweat as he kept up with his twin. He was lucky his father was a god and his mother a Titaness because his wounded thigh healed within seconds of Artemis pulling out the arrow. It still ached but not enough to slow him down.

"Why is she crying?" Apollo wondered.

"I don't know. Shut up and keep running," Artemis said.

When they finally reached their home, Apollo almost knocked the door off its hinge as he kicked it open.

"Mother!" he shouted.

"Mother, where are you?" Artemis stepped into the living room but she wasn't there.

They found Leto in the garden, staring out at the ocean. She saw them out the corner of her eye and quickly wiped away her tears. She turned around and faced the twins. Leto did her best to smile.

"What happened?" Apollo was not fooled for a second by his mother's pretense.

"Nothing," she lied. Her bottom lip quivered, and she turned her attention back to the turquoise sea.

"Why were you crying, Mother?" Artemis stepped toward her.

"I'm fine," Leto said, giving them a shaky smile.

"Don't make me ask again, Mother," Artemis threatened. "I swear, I will go to the village and torture everyone until I find out why you were crying. Please . . . don't make me ask again."

"Watch your tone," Leto warned.

"Please, Mother, tell us why you're so upset," Apollo pleaded.

For a long while, Leto sat quietly, staring at the ocean as though waiting for something to pop out from beneath its salty waves.

"Do you think I'm a failure as a mother?" she whispered.

Apollo shook his head. "Of course not, why would you think such a thing?"

"I heard Niobe say that she was a better mother because she had more children than I." Leto fidgeted with the frayed ends of her skirt. "I started to cry because I wondered if it was true. What if I would've had more children with Zeus?"

"How dare she!" Artemis hissed. She balled her hands into fists, wanting to punch something. "Where is she?"

"Artemis, please don't," Leto quickly stood and pressed her cool hands on her daughter's hot cheeks.

"Where is she?" Artemis' face trembled with anger, her eyes quickly becoming bloodshot, her heart demanding revenge with every fierce beat.

Leto remained quiet.

"You" —Artemis pointed her index finger to Apollo's chest— "tell me where she is. Use your gift."

"Artemis, that's not what I use it for. Besides, it doesn't work on command."

"Tell me!" she roared.

He jumped at the ferocity behind her voice. There were times when he was greatly afraid of Artemis' temper. She was someone you wanted on your side at all times. Apollo closed his eyes and conjured up the image of Niobe. He concentrated on her face and tried to see her surroundings. It was like putting together pieces of a puzzle. At first, he didn't see anything . . . then after several moments he saw a flash of light in which he could detect the outline of Niobe's oval shaped face. Her deep-set eyes that could be both cruel and kind—depending on her mood. After another moment he heard her laughter and saw a glimpse of green. A field perhaps? Apollo wasn't sure. He concentrated harder and before he knew it, he saw Niobe and all of her children playing in a field he recognized. He had been there with Artemis when they were children. Apollo opened his eyes. He couldn't believe it had actually worked. He assumed it was the fear of getting beaten by Artemis that had sped things up. "She is in Thebes."

"Let's go," she said.

"Artemis, please." Leto grabbed her daughter's hand. "I don't want to be remembered for this. I don't want you two to be re-membered as butchers. Let it go."

"No one makes you cry, Mother. No one." Artemis pulled her hand from Leto's.

Apollo ran inside the house, went to his bedroom, and grabbed his golden bow and arrow. By the time he was outside, Artemis had already vanished. He used all of his energy to catch up to her.

"Can't wait for your brother?"

"I'm going to kill all of her children." Artemis growled, grind-ing her teeth. "I will rip off their flesh and make her wear their bones around her scrawny neck."

"I don't think death is the answer." Apollo continued to keep up with his elder sibling.

"What do you prefer?" She came to a sudden stop. "Would you rather see Mother crying every day? Would you rather Mother be upset all of the time because some wanton harlot cannot keep her legs closed?"

"No, of course not," Apollo replied.

"We made a vow long ago, you and I. We swore we wouldn't let her suffer. Are you going to back out on your word? Because if you are, then by all means go home, little brother. I have hunted larger, more dangerous game. I don't need you."

Apollo sighed, remembering the promise he had made long ago with his twin. "Yes, I remember."

"What do you suggest we do? Seeing as death makes you queasy all of a sudden?" She crossed her arms across her chest.

"Killing them all is a bit much . . . Why don't we let two of them live?"

"A boy and a girl?"

"Yes," he replied.

"Interesting." Artemis looked off into the distance. She was seriously considering Apollo's suggestion.

"You can choose whomever you want to spare. I don't really care. We can make it so Niobe and mother are equal," he suggested.

Artemis gave him a quick grin and a gentle nudge on the shoulder. "I like the way you think, brother. Let's go." She took off running before Apollo could give her a reply.

They sped off to Thebes where they found Niobe sitting under a tree, watching her sons play and wrestle on the ground. Her daughters were across the field, making flower crowns and chains and giggling at a joke that the youngest sister was telling.

Apollo stood and watched the scene before him. Niobe was a beautiful woman—there was no doubt about that. She had jet-black hair that cascaded down her back in long luscious waves with eyes the color of dark honey. Her lips gave way to an easy smile as she watched her sons tumbling on the green grass. All fourteen of her children looked like her in one way or another.

"Seven daughters and seven sons . . . she's a bloody whore," Artemis hissed.

"You take care of the daughters, I'll take care of the sons," Apollo said.

"With pleasure."

When Apollo turned to his sister, she was long gone. The only trace that she left behind was the lingering scent of bark and jasmine.

Apollo grabbed an arrow, pulled back the bowstring, and aimed it at Niobe's eldest son, Agenor. Apollo closed his eyes and looked away. He wasn't like his sister, who enjoyed the thrill of the hunt. She reveled in taking a life if it were for the right reason. Apollo didn't feel the same way. Even though he felt they deserved to die, he still couldn't bear the thought of seeing the look on the boy's face as he realized he was dying. Nor could he bear the sight of Niobe's face as she watched her children die before her eyes.

"Zeus," Leto whispered.

She waited a few moments. Nothing. Not even the wind stirred the blades of grass.

"Fool. Why would he remember you?" She chastised herself. "It's been twelve years. He's probably seducing some young nubile woman in a far-off field somewhere."

"I'm sorry to disappoint you, but I did all of my seducing yesterday," a deep male voice spoke.

A soft breath escaped her lips when she turned around and found Zeus standing behind her. She couldn't help but smile at the sight of him. He was still the most handsome man she had ever laid eyes on. He took a step toward her and placed his large, warm hands on her cool, pale shoulders, slowly drawing her close to his body, taking in the scent of petrichor that came from him.

"Every day I wonder, *Is today the day she will finally call for me? Will she whisper my name?* And after years of waiting, my heart stirred to finally hear my name from your lips," he whispered.

She beamed at his words. She often wondered if he had forgotten her, and now she finally knew the truth.

He kissed her on the forehead. "Now tell me . . . why have you called me?"

"Do you know what your children are doing right now?"

"Yes," he replied.

"And?"

"They're being far too kind." He chuckled.

"They're killing innocent children," she protested.

"She shouldn't have compared her children to those belonging to a god," he said.

"But . . ."

"She shouldn't have made you cry." He scoffed.

"Is that what this is about?"

"I . . ." He took a deep breath and regained his composure. "I would have killed Niobe, her children . . . her entire family when I first caught sight of your tears. You are lucky Artemis and Apollo acted as quickly as they did."

"But innocent children are going to die," she argued.

"You have a soft heart, my love. Innocent people die all the time. The Moirae cut the string blindfolded for a reason. They don't care who is guilty, innocent, old, or young. All they know is that the string must be cut."

"The children . . ." She sobbed.

"There will be more to replace the ones she's lost. She's a fertile, loose woman," he said.

"Don't say such things," she whispered.

"Leto . . . my beautiful," he said, caressing her cheek. "Everything happens for a reason. Reasons that even I cannot control. Apollo and Artemis have started a chain of events that will lead them to their destiny, and I would be sorely disappointed if you or I got in the way of the greatness that lies ahead of them."

Leto sighed and didn't argue with him about it anymore.

ARTEMIS SMILED WHEN SHE heard Niobe's screams. She shot poison-tipped arrows at six of her daughters. She watched as the life slowly escaped their once glittering and shimmering eyes, leaving nothing but darkness and a vast emptiness. Artemis walked up to Niobe who was sobbing and rocking the dead body of her eldest son in her arms.

"Pride is an ugly sin," she said. "And that is what killed your children. We left you your youngest son and daughter so that you will be reminded to be humble in the presence of gods."

Artemis then leaned over and pulled out the arrow that jutted from Agenor's chest and tossed it on Niobe's lap. "Melt it. Turn it into a chain and wear it around your neck everyday so you will be reminded of your sin and what it cost you."

Niobe only gave Artemis a vacant stare and cried.

Artemis turned and walked away, satisfied with what she and her brother had accomplished that afternoon.

"That was a bit overdramatic, don't you think?" Apollo mused.

"I think it was perfectly appropriate."

"And what was that bit about gods? We're not gods. We have to eat the blessed ambrosia on Mount Olympus, by Zeus, in order for us to be gods. And as long as Hera is there, that won't ever happen."

"Niobe doesn't know that," she argued.

"Yes, but our father hears everything, even when he's not really paying that much attention," he said.

"He loves Mother far too much to lay a finger on us. Don't worry."

"Who's worried? Our father is only the God of Gods, Wielder

of Lightning, Storm Bringer, God of Justice, and father to half the world. I'm certainly *not* worried." His sarcasm was stronger than he'd intended.

"Shut-up," Artemis said as she pushed him away, making him fall on the ground.

Apollo and Artemis arrived home, covered in sweat, their clothes splattered in blood.

"I see that the ghastly deed is done," Leto said as soon as she caught sight of her children.

"Yes," Artemis replied.

"Very well. Go and bathe. You both reek of death."

They quietly bowed their heads and did as they were told.

Several days later, Leto took a small boat from Delos to the mainland, as she did each week. She went to a little village not far from the shore in order to get fruits and vegetables that she couldn't grow on the soil in her garden. It was an outing Leto looked forward to since it could get quite lonely on the island. And occasionally talking to Delos didn't count as a social interaction.

Leto hummed to herself as she inspected a light green pear. She could already imagine herself biting into it and feeling the grainy, sweet fruit against her tongue. She smiled and placed it in her basket, ready to grab a few more when someone bumped against her shoulder.

"Excuse me," she whispered.

The short, angry-looking woman "harumphed" as she scurried away.

Leto stared after the woman and shook her head in confusion. *That was strange.*

She moved on to the vendor selling the figs and dates, they were Artemis' favorite. Just as she was about to start bargaining with the merchant, Leto heard the whisperings of a small group of women next to her.

"Have you heard?"

"Niobe?"

"She hasn't stopped crying."

"Apollo and Artemis did it."

"Twelve children dead."

"Murdered."

"Butchers."

"Niobe is still crying."

"She won't come down the mountain."

That was all Leto heard the entire morning. She picked her items at the vendors and made her way back home as fast as she could.

"Apollo! Artemis!" she cried, slamming the door behind her.

"What's wrong?" Apollo ran from his bedroom.

"Where is your sister?"

"Hunting," he replied.

Leto sighed and ran her fingers nervously through her hair.

"What's wrong?" he repeated, noticing how distressed his mother looked. *Why can't people just leave her alone?*

Leto finally calmed herself and sat. She explained to her son what she had heard in the village that day.

"It's just gossip. People will eventually forget about it." He tried his best to ease his mother's worries.

"Forget?" The anger evident on her face. "*Forget?*"

"We're not anyone of great importance, Mother," he said.

"No one of great importance? Have you forgotten who your *father* is? Need I remind you of how you and your sister came into existence?" She stood to her full height, looking like the Titan that she was. "Need I remind you who I am?"

Apollo was always afraid of his mother when she got like this. He never knew the full extent of her powers. She masked them well. It also helped that his mother was kind and had no reason to want to flaunt her powers the way the other Titans did. He had seen her truly angry once and that day the earth beneath her feet had dried as though a great drought had passed through their lands. He knew of his father's temper and what to expect. It was his mother Apollo feared to anger.

"Forgive me, Mother," he said.

Leto steadied her breathing and did her best to steady her emotions. She knew what she was capable of doing when she used her powers. It would be catastrophic. If she lost control for more than a minute, women for miles would become barren, trees would wither and die, rivers would dry up, and animals would die. That was why she always did her best to remain pleasant, to keep her temper in check. This was why she avoided drama and gossip.

"Go find your sister," Leto snapped, but quickly covered her mouth with both of her hands the moment the words escaped her lips, regretting the tone she had used with her dear son. Her mouth tasted like ash. She whispered, "I just want to be left alone for a while."

"Yes, mother." Apollo scrambled out the door in search of his twin.

CHAPTER 8

LETO WENT INTO HER BEDROOM, SETTLED INTO HER BED, and closed her eyes. She felt as though the world around her was falling apart. She thought about her children and how their lives would soon change.

I can't really call them children. Apollo already looks more like a man each time I look at him, and Artemis' has been itching to go further and further away from home the more she hunts.

Leto fell into a deep sleep with these thoughts running rampant through her mind. When she opened her eyes, she found herself in a dream world. Zeus appeared before her. She smiled warily at him, unsure as to why she was here in the first place.

"It is time," he said.

"Time for what?"

"I'm giving them a gift," he stated.

"What sort of gift?" She frowned, worried; Zeus often

gave gifts that couldn't be refused. Things that couldn't be given back once gifted.

"Godhood," he said.

"No, please don't. I'll never see them," she pleaded. Even though they were already gods being children of Zeus . . . it wouldn't be official until they've eaten the sacred ambrosia. Then they would be assigned the elements that would be under their command on earth. They wouldn't stay in Delos. They wouldn't need her anymore. She would be completely alone.

"This isn't something I'm asking of you. I'm simply telling you what must be," Zeus said.

Leto wept, but this time her tears couldn't sway him. Apollo and Artemis would be in Olympus, and nothing Leto said or did would change it.

"No!" She gasped and sat up from her bed, covered in sweat. "NO!" she screamed as she released her power and let it course red-hot through her veins. She multiplied in size. Before she knew it, she was her full height of fifty feet, with a hole in her roof.

ARTEMIS HAD HER EYE SET on a stag. She had been following it all morning and had finally caught up to it. She imagined the delicious scent of cooked meat wafting through the house and the steam that would caress her cheek as she grilled the meat on an open flame. She smiled as she pulled the bowstring back. She was just about to release her arrow when she heard her brother call out her name.

"Artemis!" he cried.

The stag ran away.

"Bastard," she hissed. "Where are you?" She scanned the forest for her twin brother.

She found him easily. He was making more noise than a parrot—breaking branches, rustling every leaf he came in contact with, and calling out her name. She released her silver arrow and willed it to strike him in the chest.

"Art—" He was silenced the moment he felt the sharp end of his sister's arrow. "Damn it, Artemis! Why must you riddle me with arrows time and time again?"

"Because, brother, you make noise that causes me to lose my game," Artemis said. "Who do you think catches the meat we eat every day? I do. Who cooks it? I do. What the hell do you do all damned day? Nothing. Not a damned thing. So guess what, little brother? You owe me and Mother a stag just as big as the one I was about to catch."

"This is ridiculous. I do nothing? I meditate and use my gift of prophecy to help you, Mother, and everyone around us." Apollo stared at the arrow jutting from his chest.

"Everyone around us? You mean the three people that Delos allows to visit the island?" Artemis teased.

"They count."

"All you do is have visions of the same girl. The one with green hair you have told me about time and time again. And there is no one on this world that fits that description," Artemis said.

"She is real." Apollo's voice was a little too loud for his own taste.

But Artemis was correct. No matter how hard he tried not to, he saw that girl with the green hair every single day. He tried to avoid the visions. But no amount of meditating about more important things, he saw her. He shook his head and forced himself back to the present. He had other things to worry about.

"Do you mind?" He pointed to the arrow sticking out of his chest.

"I do." She smiled viciously.

"Fine." Apollo grabbed the end of the arrow and pushed it further through his chest. He winced in pain as he reached behind and yanked the arrow out of his back. "Here." He panted as he handed Artemis her bloodstained arrow.

"Now . . . why have you come here and interrupted my hunt?"

"Mother is upset." He gazed at the wound in his chest, watching it heal.

"Why? What happened?"

"Gossip. The people in the village are still talking about what we did," he explained.

"She need not worry about such things." Artemis waved her hand, dismissing her brother's words and worries.

"Mother was this close to unleashing her powers to the fullest." He held his thumb and index finger only a fraction apart from each other. "I think that is cause enough to worry. Remember what happened the last time Mother was angry?"

Artemis shuddered. "How could I forget?"

Apollo parted his lips to say something else, but before he could utter a word, the earth began to tremble and quake beneath their feet. The twins looked into each other's eyes in alarm.

"Mother," they said in unison.

They sped through the woods, their limbs moving in time. Anyone looking at them from a distance would have thought them a two-headed beast, for their bodies moved in perfect synchronization.

LETO GASPED AS SHE STUDIED her body. She hadn't expected to make a hole in her house. Then again, she hadn't expected a lot of things in her life to turn out the way they did. The last time she was her normal height was when Zeus was young and had recently become leader of the gods. She looked up at the sky, cursing the clouds and the god who lived among them. In the distance, she could see Mount Olympus. She decided to go straight to the source of her despair. She would go to the palace of the gods and convince Zeus, the Oracle, and the Moirae themselves if she had to, that taking her children away from her would be the worst possible thing to do.

What would I do without them? How could I possibly exist without my children by my side? Before they came, all my life was nothing but a blur. The moment I laid eyes on Apollo and Artemis, everything changed. Everything made sense. My vision cleared. What will become of me once they are gone?

"What about me? WHAT ABOUT ME?" Her voice changed from a mutter to a shout.

Her voice echoed through the land, scaring birds out of their nests. Schools of fish swam away from the sound. Trees stood still, and the leaves darkened. Leto's breath quickened as she imagined all of the things she wanted to say to Zeus. With a newly found determination, she made her way to Mount Olympus.

HERA WAS ENJOYING A VERY rare, quiet afternoon with her husband. It had been many years since they'd had a day together where they weren't arguing, cursing or throwing things at each other. She was . . . bored. Hera wished for a tiny bit of excitement but she didn't want it to be her fault. She didn't want to be the one to blame for disrupting their peace. She glanced over her shoulder to see what Zeus was doing, and he looked equally bored. He kept throwing random challenges at the man inside their miniature coliseum, and no matter what he did, the mortal overcame all of the challenges.

"Bah!" He huffed.

In the distance, Hera heard a soft 'boom.' She frowned. "Did you hear that?"

"That was me," he said.

"No, it was something else . . . in the distance." She frowned. Boom!

"That sound," she said.

"Nothing I can't handle, I'm sure," he replied.

Hera smiled inwardly. She had a feeling that today was going to be one of those days when Zeus would be the one in an uncomfortable position. She walked from the throne room and laughed once she stepped out onto the balcony. A fifty-foot Leto marched straight toward the palace. She didn't look happy at all. Hera laughed harder.

"What's so funny?" Zeus stepped outside. He frowned at his laughing wife. It was a rare thing to hear her giggle with such careless glee.

"See what happens when you sleep with someone who isn't mortal? They fight back when you least expect it." She pointed to Leto.

Zeus couldn't believe it. His beautiful Leto was fifty feet tall and looked as though she wanted to crush everything beneath her feet. A fully fledged Titan in all of her glory. Even he was surprised at her transformation. He'd been incredibly impressed with the control she'd maintained over her powers during their lovemaking. He'd never realized how strong she was until now. How blind he had been not to see it. But that wasn't the only thing that captured Zeus' attention.

I would love to be in her bosom right now.

"We need to talk." Leto's voice was loud and thunderous.

"Of course." Zeus gave her a wide smile. He shook his head, whispering, "My beautiful."

She had been perfect all along. She was always meant to be the mother of his twins.

APOLLO AND ARTEMIS ARRIVED to a destroyed home. The roof was completely gone—pieces of it surrounded their humble home—and the walls were now piles of rubble.

"Mother's room is in complete shambles," Apollo said.

"She's nowhere to be found. Where could she be? Do you think someone came in and took her?"

Apollo studied the rubble and the trail of destruction left behind by Leto's unknown kidnapper. "Whoever did this went straight to Mount Olympus."

Artemis sighed heavily. "Let's go."

"You don't sound that thrilled," Apollo teased. "Normally, you're always up for another adventure."

"Slaying mortals and wild beasts is not the same as knocking on the door that belongs to the house of the gods," she said.

"Then what do you suggest?" Apollo arched his eyebrow.

"Go knock on Father's door, what else?"

"Very well," he said.

They gathered their things and went to their father's house, hoping to find their mother or at least some answers.

"Leto, why don't you control yourself and come inside?" Zeus motioned toward the palace.

"I'm not going in there."

"Believe me, Hera won't do anything to you," he said.

"I'm not afraid of her. I don't care anymore."

"Leto . . ."

Leto pounded her fist to the ground and shouted, "I've controlled myself long enough! It's time you listened to what *I* have to say. How could you?"

Zeus said nothing.

"How could you think that I would let you take them from me without a fight?"

"Leto, you don't know what you're fighting. This is something that's bigger than us and you know it," he said.

"It's so easy for you, isn't it? To plant your seed in every womb you find. You didn't carry them in your belly for nine months. You didn't push them into this world. You didn't care for them all these years, feed them, clean them, dry their tears, cure their ills, worry about whether they were happy or sad."

"Yes, I did," he replied.

"No! You didn't. Don't lie to me. You were seducing some woman or man, you . . . you . . ." She panted, unable to finish her sentence. Her face slowly turned red. *Bastard. You damned bastard. Why did you leave me?* That's what she wanted to say. Those were the words she wanted to throw at him, but she couldn't utter a sound. All she could do was choke on that sentence and push it back down her throat.

"What will you have me do? Turn you and the children into mortals?" Zeus suggested. "You will lead a peaceful life then, but I can assure you that you will be forgotten. Your grandchildren will speak kindly of you and then no more. Your name will die on their lips. If you let the twins become gods of Mount Olympus, they will bring a much-needed balance to this world."

"What are you saying?"

"Artemis is to be goddess of the moon and all things that roam in the darkness, and Apollo will be god of the sun and all things that glow from within," Zeus said.

Leto was speechless. She didn't think it would be something as grand as what he was describing. It made sense that Apollo should be the god of the sun, he was always in such good spirits, even when things went sour. Immediately, she regretted the tone she had taken with Apollo the last time they spoke. She would have to make him his favorite dish to make up for her fiery outburst.

"But Artemis loves to hunt and run about in the forest," she whispered.

"She will be goddess of that as well if that is what she wishes. She will be worshipped by women as well as men," he said.

For the second time in her life, his words hypnotized her.

Me . . . Leto . . . mother to the god of the sun and the goddess of the moon.

"Mother?"

Leto spun around when she heard the sound of her daughter's voice calling out her name.

Within moments, Leto shrank to the size that everyone was accustomed to seeing. Her children towered over her once more. She was back to being *small, defenseless* Leto, no longer a dangerous Titan. Instead, she was merely a mother trying to hang on to her children for a while longer.

"My children," she whispered, her eyes watering. She then fell to the ground and sobbed.

Apollo raced toward her and wrapped his arms around her.

"Are you all right?" His eyes darted from Leto to Zeus. His blue eyes accused his father of crimes he knew he would commit in the near future.

She took a deep breath. "Yes. I'm fine, darling." She wiped the tears with the back of her hand and stood.

"What did you do to her?" Apollo demanded of his father.

"You know just as well as I that I am innocent. I have not laid a finger on your mother, so do not look at me with those angry eyes," Zeus warned, "or you might find them looking at the bottom of the ocean."

"What's going on here?" Artemis narrowed her eyes.

"Your Mother and I were having a discussion about your future. And I think it's time I gave you some additional gifts to help you in this new path you are to take," Zeus explained.

"What sort of gifts?" A deep frown formed between Apollo's brows. He was always suspicious of anything that came from his father.

"Apollo, you and your sister are to be made into gods. I think it's time people know you are my children."

They smiled. This was certainly not what they had expected when they made their way up to Mount Olympus. They knew that once they were gods, no one would dare risk an offense from them. Now everyone would leave their mother alone, which was the only thing they wanted.

"Thank you, Father," Artemis said.

Apollo overcame his initial shock seconds after his sister spoke and thanked his father as well. Apollo glanced at his mother; it seemed to him that she thought the world around her, as she knew, it was crumbling.

And it will change, he thought. He knew that once they ate the ambrosia, they would have to leave Leto behind. The twins would have their own lives to lead and their own responsibilities once they came to their powers.

"Who destroyed the house?" Artemis demanded.

"Yes, who?" Apollo echoed her.

"Did father kidnap you?" Artemis looked to Zeus.

"No, it was me. I destroyed the house," Leto confessed.

"Why?" Apollo placed a hand on his mother's shoulders.

"That doesn't matter anymore," she said, not wanting to let them know that she had been against this decision all along, that she wanted to be selfish and risk them becoming mortal for the sake of keeping them to herself.

Selfish Leto. The world must know them so that they too can feel love from hands other than your own. She lifted her gaze to Zeus. "When will the ceremony take place?"

"By the next full moon. Make sure you are here as the sun sets," Zeus explained.

"Do we need to bring anything for sacrifice?" Artemis smiled, already her eyes twinkling and shimmering at the thought of catching a bear or some wild beast that would finally give her some sort of challenge.

Zeus smiled and shook his head. "Not for this, my dear."

Artemis looked crestfallen.

"It really won't be necessary, but . . . once you are a goddess, you can have mortals and priests leave sacrifices for you." He promised.

Artemis brightened up at that prospect. Zeus took a moment to steal a glance at Leto; he wanted to see if she would protest once more. But all she did was glare at him.

Don't make this harder than it has to be, he whispered into her mind.

"They will be here," Leto said. "I promise you that."

"I know," Zeus said.

CHAPTER 9

Artemis' ceremony took place during the full moon. She arrived at sunset as her father had requested. Dressed in a long white toga, with her black hair combed and plainly styled for the first time in several months, she actually looked like the beautiful young woman she was—the goddess she was to become.

A priestess offered Artemis the ambrosia, presented to her in thin, peach-colored slices on a golden plate. Her fingers trembled slightly as she reached out to grab one sliver of the immortal fruit and slipped it into her mouth. She was surprised at its sweetness. She half expected it to taste like something that had been buried underground for several centuries for some strange reason.

She gazed at the moon she would command for the rest of her days as the fruit of the gods went down her throat. She felt a soft hum course through her veins. She panted and gasped for air as she felt her body becoming hot and cold all at once.

Artemis' body broke into a cold sweat and she began to fall, but Zeus grabbed her before she fell to the floor.

"You're changing into your new self from the inside out," he whispered. "It will pass in a few more moments."

Artemis shook her head and struggled to breathe.

I'm dying. He tricked me, she thought as she accused her father of murder with her gaze. No matter how hard she stared, Zeus' face remained calm throughout the entire struggle. Suddenly, the pain and the paralyzing feeling went away. She felt powerful, as if she could move several mountains with a single push.

"I would never hurt you," Zeus said as he stood and helped his daughter to her feet. "Tell your brother to be here by sunrise. Tell him nothing of what happened to you tonight."

"Why?"

"Because he needs to experience this for himself, and you can't protect him for the rest of his life," Zeus said.

Artemis nodded, understanding what her father meant. Apollo was always being coddled for some reason, but Artemis didn't mind because it meant she could run off and do whatever she wanted. No one ever dared say no to her, and now that she was a goddess, no one would ever be able to stop her.

"Goodbye, Father, and thank you." Artemis embraced Zeus for the first time since she was a child and vanished.

Artemis sped down the mountain where her mother and her brother were anxiously waiting for her.

Leto looked at her daughter and noticed the immediate change in her. She looked taller, her back straighter, shoulders broader. Her muscles rippled beneath her pale and shimmering skin.

Her hair was shining in a way Leto had never seen before. Leto thought about bowing before her, but she knew Artemis wouldn't tolerate that.

"Father will see you just before sunrise," Artemis said to Apollo.

Even her voice is different, Leto noted. Before she could part her lips and utter a sound, Artemis was gone.

She's gone forever, Leto thought as she watched her daughter run off toward the horizon. The only thing Artemis left behind was the dust her feet had kicked up into the air.

"She seemed different, Mother," Apollo said.

"I know, darling. I know," Leto replied.

"I won't do it unless you want me to," he whispered.

Leto gave him a sad smile. It was always like him to try to make her happy, but she promised herself she wouldn't be selfish. She ran her fingers through his golden hair, cupped his chin, and kissed him on the cheek.

"You will go to your father before the sun rises, and you will take the ambrosia. It is your destiny, my son," she said.

Apollo nodded and did as his mother asked. Slowly, he made his way up the mountain and climbed to Olympus, a place that would soon become his home.

Apollo's sandaled feet felt the rocks beneath his calloused soles. He thought of his mother and everything he and his sister had done to protect her. As he got closer to the palace, he knew this would be the only way he could keep her safe for all times. As soon as he was a god, no one would dare touch her or speak ill of her. With that in mind, he quickened his pace.

"FOR A MOMENT, I THOUGHT you had changed your mind," Zeus said when he saw his son enter the throne room.

"I was enjoying the view," he replied.

"The sun will rise in a few moments. Are you sure you want to take the ambrosia?" Zeus asked. "Once you do, there is no turning back. You will never die no matter how hard you try to end your own life."

"It sounds to me that you are speaking from experience."

Zeus' eyes darkened as he remembered all the times he had tried to kill himself when he was younger. Nothing he had done had worked. He had been raised to be terrified of his father Cronus who, in order to maintain control, ate his own children. Young Zeus had preferred to see Death by his own hand rather than spend an eternity inside his father's stomach.

He gave Apollo a tight-lipped smile. "That is a conversation for another occasion."

Apollo nodded.

A veiled priestess dressed in white appeared and handed him a golden chalice filled to the brim with ambrosia.

"I thought it was a fruit," Apollo said.

"It's different for each person. Ambrosia has no true shape in the material world. It just *is*," Zeus explained.

Apollo took the chalice from the priestess who sighed and vanished like a fog the moment the golden cup left her hands. Apollo took a deep breath and watched as the bright yellow sun broke through the mountains, filling the room with soft orange light. He drank the ambrosia. It was sweet; it tasted like strawberries, pears, and grapes.

Zeus waited for his son to collapse and struggle with his change the way Artemis had, but that didn't happen. Instead, his son glowed bright and shined like the sun that was slowly rising to the sky. He heard a hum coming from his son's body and watched as a golden cord sprouted from Apollo's chest, dancing its way toward the sun. Surprised, Apollo stared at his father with a questioning look but couldn't get the words out of his mouth. All he could do was close his eyes and accept the change that was taking place.

In that moment, Zeus knew that Apollo would be one of the greatest gods in the world.

APOLLO BLINKED. ONE moment he was himself and then the next, he was a new person. Completely transformed. He was still Apollo . . . only a better version. Faster, stronger, smarter, brighter, better . . . always better. He felt an invisible string connect his heart to the rising sun. He now commanded that shining orb in the sky. He thought of all the things he could do. He closed his eyes and saw his sister dancing through the forest, drunk with power. He also saw his mother, Leto still waiting for him, wringing her hands anxiously. He remembered all of the visions he had seen early in his life. His mother running from the black python. His mother crying. Leto screaming in pain as she gave birth to him on the island of Delos. The girl with the dark green hair. But his thoughts always went back to the slithering reptile and its forked tongue.

"What's the serpent's name and where can I find it?" was the first thing out of his mouth after his divine transformation.

"Why do you ask?" Zeus knew Apollo spoke of Hera's pet python, Kiril.

"Because I'm going to kill it," he replied.

"Apollo," Zeus began, "I don't mean to tell you what to do. You are a man now . . . a god more importantly, but I don't believe it is wise to anger Hera. She is very easy to upset. Her vengeance knows no limits."

"Father, forgive me, but Mother must be avenged for all she suffered while she carried Artemis and me in her womb. It's not fair. It wasn't her fault. She didn't deserve it."

Zeus looked at his glowing son. He couldn't argue with him. Hera had sent Kiril to do her dirty work. The dark creature wandered throughout the world and caused chaos wherever it slithered, leaving destruction and death behind. Zeus told Apollo where he could find Kiril and promised that he would deal with Hera later.

APOLLO TRAVELED TO DELPHI. Zeus had said that Kiril would be close to the Castalian Spring, where he made his home. Night fell before he finally found Kiril. Apollo watched from the shadows as Kiril wrapped his onyx body around a struggling calf. The poor creature kicked and mooed for its mother. The python tightened its grip the harder the calf fought. Apollo couldn't watch any more of this brutal and savage murder.

"Enough!" Apollo bellowed.

Kiril hissed as his eyes locked on Apollo's form. His tongue danced out of his mouth as he took in the scent of the newly anointed god. He didn't release the calf. Instead, he tightened his grip even more. His black, soulless eyes stared at Apollo as though challenging him to do something about how he prepared his meals.

Apollo drew one of his golden arrows and shot it at Kiril. The python was just as quick as the arrow; he twisted his body so that the calf was exposed and the arrow struck the poor creature in the neck.

"You monster," Apollo mumbled. He hadn't expected the python to be intelligent.

Kiril released the calf as he hissed softly, the sound equivalent to a snake's laugh. Apollo pulled out several arrows and shot them all, one by one. Kiril dodged each arrow with the fluidity and ease of water.

How can something that causes so much pain move so smoothly?

Apollo shot another series of arrows at the python until one finally struck the black reptile on the back. Kiril's eyes glowed red for a fraction of a second before the snake let out an angry hiss. Apollo grinned as he pulled out his sword. He had been waiting a long time to slice off Kiril's head.

After hours of fighting each other. Apollo finally delivered a deadly blow to Kiril's neck. The python's headless body thrashed, and dark red blood gushed from the mortal wound.

"May you rot and never know peace you retched beast," Apollo said. "My mother is now avenged."

He grabbed Kiril's head and tossed it in a sack. It was his new trophy.

Many years later . . .

"Master Apollo," Eos whispered softly into his ear.

Apollo opened his eyes. He smiled, his blue gaze falling upon his beautiful servant. Her olive-toned skin was tanned from all the time she spent out in the sun she loved so much. Her eyes were bright green with shimmering tones of amber sprinkled here and there. It was as though someone had captured the morning sunlight shining upon a new leaf and placed that color inside her eyes.

Opening his eyes each morning wasn't such a hardship with Eos there to greet him. Even though he wanted to stay in bed a little longer, that simply wouldn't do. The world was counting on him to make the sun rise, to light the world so that crops could grow. People believed everything would be good with the universe as long the sun took its place in the sky each day.

"Make the announcement," he said.

"As you wish." Eos bowed her head and walked away without making a sound. He watched her dark brown curls softly bounce upon her back, her salmon dress fluttering and floating behind her like a butterfly softly flapping its wings.

"Today is going to be a perfect day," Apollo whispered.

ARTEMIS WATCHED AS THE sun rose. Eos did her job and announced Apollo's arrival to the world. The sky was tinted peach, pink, purple, and light blue, each color more breathtakingly beautiful than the last.

Artemis had to hand it to her brother; he certainly made a show out of bringing light into the world every day. Each morning was different, no sunrise the same as the last. There was no comparison. The grass beneath her feet was bright green, as though illuminated from the inside out. Morning dew covered each blade. As the sunlight struck each drop of water, the fields glimmered and sparkled like diamonds as far as the eye could see.

She wasn't sure she could do that with the moon. No one noticed how bright the moon shined when it was full or how the stars sparkled and shimmered more when her silver orb was high in the dark velvet sky. It wasn't that she lacked creativity, it was just that she didn't put in as much effort as she would like. No one knew that the moon was a mirror to the sun, reflecting the sun's light onto the world. No one noticed. Sure, there were a few things she could do differently, but no one ever welcomed the night the way she did. Everything was always unclear in the darkness—too many shadows, too many things that could not be seen, too many things that were unknown, and, naturally, mankind was afraid of everything it did not know.

"Good job little, brother," she whispered, "you have managed to outdo me once more."

Artemis retreated back to her room.

WHILE APOLLO RODE HIS golden chariot, he looked down at the world below. His horses breathed fire across the sky, leaving a line of flames for the sun to follow as it made its way across the heavens throughout the day. People were already rising, greeting the sun with a warm smile and kindness in their eyes. Their nightmares and worries vanishing once he brought the daylight.

Just as he was about to look straight ahead and go about his daily routine, he saw her out of the corner of his eye. He focused his attention and got a closer look at the beauty in the river. His heart fluttered at the sight of her.

Hello, little one, and who might you be? He wondered.

For a moment, he thought her hair was black, but once the sunlight shone upon her locks, he noticed it was hunter green.

It was she. The girl from his visions. The one he had been seeing for as long as he could remember. There was no mistaking the green hair.

I swear on the River Styx, I will find out who you are, little one.

DAPHNE GASPED AS SHE FELT the first cold splash of water on her face. "Stop doing that," she shrieked to her sister, Stilbe.

"Stop doing that," Stilbe mimicked as she continued throwing water.

Daphne couldn't help but giggle at Stilbe's poor imitation of her. She bit her bottom lip and immediately wished she hadn't laughed. All it would do was encourage her to do it again.

"How are you ever to find a husband if you continue to act like a child?" Daphne scolded her sister.

"He will just have to fall in love with my undeniable charm." Stilbe fluttered her eyelashes playfully.

"My calloused foot has more charm than you, sister."

Stilbe gasped and pretended to be offended. "How cruel you are to me. Such terrible words you use against your little sister."

"You don't know what cruelty is, my dear Stilbe," Daphne said.

"Why such sullen words? Are you not looking forward to leaving home and exploring the world beyond Father's realm?"

Daphne became pensive as she absentmindedly played with a lock of her hair. "I don't know. I'm not certain if I want things to change. Why should they? Why can't I just stay here and help Father take care of the river that bears his name? Why must I marry the first man who might fill my head with nonsense and carry his children?"

"Are you saying you do not wish to marry at all?" Stilbe's surprise was evident on her face. She stared at Daphne with her dark brown eyes as though looking at her for the first time . . . as if unsure who Daphne was anymore.

"I want to be free like Artemis," Daphne said, her olive eyes becoming glassy as she imagined herself running and hunting with her favorite goddess. "I want no man to own me. I want to be able to go wherever I please and answer to no one."

"Isn't that a bit lonely?" Stilbe tilted her head.

"Sometimes." Daphne shrugged. "I want to be alone."

"Do you not want my company then? Am I not good enough to stand by your side?" Stilbe tried to hide the tears that were seconds away from falling down her cheek. She wiped a renegade tear with the back of her hand and wished to be able to understand her eldest sister.

"Stilbe, I will always need my sister. I will always want you by my side. It's strangers and strange men who worry me."

"What if you meet a handsome and gentle man? Why not give someone like that the opportunity to win your heart?"

"Men like that don't exist," Daphne replied.

"Father is handsome and gentle."

"He is the exception to the rule," Daphne said.

"You are strange." Stilbe threw up her hands in mock surrender. "Nothing I say or do will change the way you feel, am I correct?"

Daphne gave her a sad smile and nodded.

"Now the other nymphs will make fun of me because they will think I am as queer as you." Stilbe splashed Daphne in the face with a handful of water.

"Who are you calling queer, you sneaky little minx?" Daphne chased Stilbe and pushed her into the river. They spent the rest of the afternoon playing and giggling in their father's domain.

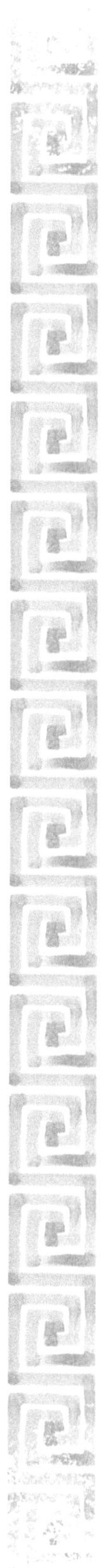

CHAPTER 10

"WHO IS SHE?" APOLLO POINTED TO THE GIRL IN THE RIVER from his home up in the mountains.

"Who?" Eos squinted, trying to see to whom he was pointing.

"That girl in the river . . . with the green hair."

"Oh, that's Daphne. She's the daughter of Peneus, the river god, and the nymph Ladon."

Apollo closed his eyes. He had a vision of him kissing her. His manhood throbbed at the thought of her soft lips pressed against his. He could smell the sweet water that still lingered on her skin. He wanted to take a closer look at her, but it would have to wait until later.

He had some place he needed to be.

"This shouldn't take long," he mumbled as he walked out the door. "I want you to keep a close eye on Daphne. When I return, I want you to tell me everything you know about her."

"Of course," Eos said, bowing her head.

As soon as Apollo left, Eos let out a heavy sigh and studied the beautiful nymph, wondering, *What does he see in her that he does not see in me?* She watched and studied every move, gesture, and facial expression Daphne made. With any luck, the nymph would only be another heartbreak for Apollo. Eos hoped that he would turn to her once it happened. She wanted to be the one to mend his shattered heart this time.

I got rid of Hyacinthus, she thought. *I can certainly get rid of Daphne.*

Hyacinthus was a handsome youth with whom Apollo had fallen in love. Eos had to admit, she had never seen anyone with eyes that were such a deep purple. She hated the way Apollo and Hyacinthus stared at each other day in and day out as though they were the answer to each other's prayers. In a moment of jealousy, Eos had asked her son Zephyrus to help her.

"Mother, I would prefer not to meddle in these kinds of affairs," he had said. "Ask Notus, he has a hot temper and likes to cause trouble."

"Do this for me and I swear on the River Styx I will never ask anything of you ever again," Eos said.

"You're asking me to take a life, Mother. An innocent life."

"He stands in the way of what I want," she argued.

"You always want something or someone. What makes him so different from the other men you have courted?" Her winged son eyed her curiously.

"Apollo is the god of the sun. I rise every morning for him. I have no other purpose in life."

"Isn't it enough you are the first thing he sees every morning?"

Zephyrus raised a brow at his mother. "Must you own him in the bedroom as well?"

"You don't understand," she insisted.

"I will do as you say, but don't ask me to do anything like this ever again," he'd said.

"Thank you," she had answered, smiling.

Zephyrus had flown away and quickly found Apollo and Hyacinthus playing with a discus in an empty field. They were laughing, enjoying each other's company and loving simply being together. Zephyrus had watched, unable to take his eyes from Hyacinthus. He had never seen a more beautiful young man. He'd loved the indigo eyes Hyacinthus possessed. Zephyrus couldn't understand why Apollo always had luck finding the most beautiful people in the world. Filled with the same jealousy his mother had possessed in her heart, Zephyrus had made Apollo's discus fly off course and strike poor young Hyacinthus on the head, injuring and killing Apollo's lover instantly.

Apollo had been devastated at the loss of his beloved Hyacinthus. It had taken Apollo many years to get over the loss of the handsome youth and revert to his original self . . . but there was always a reminder. On the anniversary of Hyacinthus' death, Apollo's eyes would darken; only the ghost of his normal smile would remain. Even the sun shone less bright on that day.

Eos was willing to make Apollo go through that just again so she could have him all to herself. As she stared at Daphne, she plotted different ways she could make the girl disappear.

APOLLO ARRIVED AT HIS favorite valley. It was here he kept his flock of sheep, tended by a shepherd named Ben. He was a simple fellow but sweet and trustworthy. It was something that kept the boy out of trouble and occupied. Something his mother appreciated greatly.

"What is the matter? Why have you called me here?" Apollo made his way toward Ben.

"I apologize for the disturbance, Great One, but there is something you need to see." Ben led him to an empty field and trembled when he saw the frown on Apollo's face.

"And?"

"Your sheep . . . they're all gone, Great One," he explained.

"What do you mean *gone*?" Apollo placed his hands on his hips.

Ben trembled as he looked down at the ground, too afraid to meet Apollo's gaze. "I turned my back for a few minutes to get some things I left behind, and when I returned, they were . . . gone."

"Who took them?"

"I–I don't know," Ben stammered.

"See that you find them," Apollo said.

"Yes, Great One." Ben bowed his head several times nervously and ran away.

Strange things are happening. What do The Moirae have in store for me? Apollo wondered as he made his way to the river where he was sure he could find Daphne. He wasn't sure if he was going to speak to her when he arrived, but he was certain he wanted to get a closer look at the beautiful nymph.

DAPHNE WAS ENJOYING her dinner. They had steamed sea bass, a boiled potato and olives that evening. She grabbed a lemon and squeezed its sour juices on her meal. Her hands smelled like the yellow citrus fruit. She was a little on edge that night because everyone at the table was inexplicably quiet. The only sounds were those of the soft clinks of the silverware touching the plates. Her heart jumped when she finally heard her father speak.

"Stilbe was telling me that you are not interested in getting married, Daphne." Peneus broke off a piece of his fish with his fork and chewed it slowly.

Daphne had yet to meet someone with the same intensity as her father. He was a very quiet and reserved man. She almost choked on her wine. Her vision swam as the alcohol went straight to her head. This wasn't something she was looking forward to discussing with him. It was a topic she wanted to avoid for a while, at least until Stilbe had found a mate and produced some children. Peneus was fond of children. It was one of the reasons why Daphne had so many half brothers and sisters scattered throughout the world.

Daphne's eyes quickly fell on Stilbe's dark gaze. She glared at her young sister who, sensing where their conversation was headed, grabbed her plate and left the table without excusing herself. Peneus didn't even notice, all of his attention on Daphne.

"Father . . . I don't want a man to tell me how to live my life or make me clean, wash, and bear children that may kill me." Daphne's voice was soft. Her olive eyes darted nervously from side to side. She was never sure how her father would react to the things she said.

Still waters run deep.

"That will never happen. I can protect you," he said. "Don't you have faith in your father's powers?"

"What if The Moirae decide to cut my string regardless of the protection you offer? Atropos wears a blindfold when she cuts the cord. Even the gods cannot run from her golden shears."

"I have no control over when The Moirae cut the string, my daughter," Peneus admitted, "but there is much joy to be had through marriage."

"If that is true, then why haven't you taken another wife?" As soon as the words left her mouth, she immediately wished they hadn't.

Peneus hadn't remarried since the death of Daphne and Stilbe's mother, Ladon. The moment she passed away, Peneus had turned her body into a river, which he still visited every day.

Her father looked at her, pain visible on his face. Daphne had reopened the old wound, and it stung Peneus as though someone had ripped off his flesh and doused it with salt.

"Your mother is . . . irreplaceable. To bring another woman into my home and lay down beside her would be a mockery of your mother's memory," Peneus said.

"Forgive me, Father. Please forgive your foolish daughter for taking such liberties with her loose tongue," she pleaded. "But . . . I don't want to marry. Please let me be free like the goddess Artemis." Daphne's eyes glimmered at the mention of her favorite goddess. "She hunts and keeps her virginity intact for all time. Not like Aphrodite who has it replenished every time she gives birth."

"Shh, do not speak ill of Aphrodite," he whispered, his eyes darting nervously from one end of the dining room to the next, half expecting the goddess of love to appear at any moment. Peneus was already thinking of things he could sacrifice in order to appease Aphrodite, just as a precaution.

Daphne got up from her seat and kneeled before Peneus. "Please . . . let's not talk of marriage anymore. Let me be free. That is what I want."

Peneus gazed into his daughter's eyes and saw that nothing would change her mind. No glimmer of hope. He shook his head. "I don't know why I bother arguing with you, my lovely . . . you always win."

She consistently managed to melt his heart. It wasn't in him to say no to her. The room lit up the moment she smiled at her triumph.

THE FOLLOWING DAY, APOLLO spent the entire afternoon watching Daphne from a distance. He was captivated by her natural charm and the way she moved her body. It was as though she made it her business to think before she moved a muscle. Every act was well thought out and precise . . . no mistakes.

He smiled as he conjured up the image of them kissing. He closed his eyes and willed himself back to his home.

"What can you tell me about her, Eos?"

"Anything you wish to know," she said.

Apollo took a deep breath and thought about what he wanted to know. "What is her favorite flower?"

"Phalaenopsis," she replied.

"What does it look like?" He frowned. It wasn't a flower with which he was familiar.

Eos extended her hand and, a moment later, an orchid appeared. It was pure white; he had never seen such an exquisite flower in his life. It had large, rounded petals. The only color that could be seen was a hint of yellow in the very center of the orchid.

"I have never seen anything like this." He marveled.

"It is not a common plant. Daphne saw it one day when she went to market. A traveler who had visited eastern lands brought it with him. He was so taken by her beauty that he let her keep it," Eos said.

"Find more of these for me," he commanded. "I want to fill the whole palace with this flower so that when Daphne comes to visit she will see nothing but her favorite blooms."

"As you wish." Eos vanished, leaving the orchid behind. She failed to mention the conversation she had heard between Daphne and her father. Eos also forgot to tell him of the secret vow Daphne had made to herself before she went to sleep.

I would rather die than be with a man, Daphne had sworn to herself.

"And so you shall." Eos promised.

ARTEMIS WAS IN THE MIDDLE of a field gazing up at the midnight sky. She could understand why the mortals spent most of their time studying the heavens. Some sort of answer to the hows and whys of the world had to lie in the stars. And that was one of the reasons she endeavored to get mortals to stop being so afraid of the night, to gaze into the darkened heavens the way they gazed so lovingly upon the sun and sky that came with it.

"Who would've thought astronomy would bring the moon back to its good graces?" Artemis whispered, shaking her head.

She thought about how she had felt about her brother a few days earlier and was glad that she hadn't done anything foolish. Actions driven by jealousy never ended well, and she was happy she hadn't let it cloud her judgment. Artemis took a deep breath and slowly exhaled it as she searched the skies for constellations. She would learn how to read what was in the stars. She would make it her business to know her domain better than any mortal.

EOS LET OUT A HAPPY SIGH and smiled as she gazed at her children, each one twinkling and shimmering for her. She was the mother of all the stars and planets in the universe. She was also mother to all four winds.

"It is a beautiful night, isn't it?" Apollo said as he appeared behind her.

Eos turned around and grinned at him.

"My children . . . they shine so brightly across the sky. If it hadn't taken so long and been so painful, I would happily have them all over again."

"And how are your children these days?"

Eos frowned as she concentrated, connecting with her many children. "Some thrive while others . . . I can feel when they leave this world."

This intrigued Apollo. The only beings he had connections with were Artemis and their mother. "How can you tell?"

Eos was silent for a while. She was trying to find the right words to explain the feeling of loss to a man who had nothing to lose.

"Chaos reigns in my heart days before they die. Sometimes it is fleeting, other times it lasts for months, forever leaving a gap in my heart. My children are everything to me, Apollo. They shape the world we live in. They bring peace where there is war. Love where there is hate. But I'm certain you know what I mean."

Apollo only smiled and nodded in response. He'd certainly had his fair share of lovers, but none produced any offspring, which didn't bother him at all. He didn't know if he was ready to bring children into the world, but that wasn't what he had on his mind at that moment.

"I saw her again today." He grinned.

"Who?" Eos ventured, though she knew exactly who he was talking about. *Her* again.

"Daphne," he whispered her name as though he had been thinking of her all day . . . and that *was* the case.

"Oh, yes, Daphne," Eos said.

"Did you find out anything else about her? What more can you tell me? We can pretend that I am an eager pupil and you the wise teacher." His eyes glowed at the thought of knowing some new secret about his new love interest.

Eos thought about how to answer his question. She could tell him what she'd heard Daphne promise to herself alone in the darkness.

What if that only makes him want her more? Knowing him, he would just view this as a challenge. Something after which he can chase. No . . . I can't tell him of her vows.

"She is infatuated with Eros," she blurted out.

"Really?" He sounded displeased. He found that strange, for his visions never failed him. Why would he see her face so clearly or feel her lips against his own if she weren't meant to be his? He would have to speak to Eros and find out if Daphne had approached him in any way.

"Yes." Eos' mouth tasted like ashes as she continued to lie.

It's for you. I do it for you, she told herself over and over again as she stared into Apollo's handsome face. She knew this had to be love; there was no doubt about it.

EROS THREW HIS HEAD back and moaned as he made love to Calla. The blue-haired nymph gasped as Eros' wings fluttered and twitched with his movements. She wrapped her legs around his waist, throwing her head back and letting the love that emanated from Eros wash over her.

Eros caressed her breasts. Calla couldn't believe how warm his hands were. It was as though he could do no wrong. The man could've asked her to make love in the middle of a glacier, and she would not have been able to decline his offer. It came as no great surprise to anybody. He had that effect on everyone regardless of their gender. Calla gasped again, feeling her orgasm beginning to build. Soon it would flow through her like a warm ocean. She heard a knock on the door and let out an annoyed sigh.

Whoever it is, go away. We're busy. She wanted to scream.

APOLLO MADE HIS WAY through the labyrinth of Eros' home and knocked on the love god's bedroom door. He waited, and when he didn't hear a response, he let himself into the room. He quickly understood why Eros didn't hear his knocking. He was in the middle of making love to Calla. She looked over her shoulder and gave Apollo an annoyed glance. Apollo shrugged and ignored her. It wasn't the first time he had caught one of the gods making love with one of their paramours, and it certainly wouldn't be the last.

"We need to talk," Apollo said as he averted his gaze.

Eros looked over his shoulder and groaned.

"Can it wait?" The irritation was heavy in his voice.

"It's important," Apollo said.

Eros rolled his eyes. "It always is. Can you wait until I'm finished at least? I'm almost ready to climax, and you standing there doesn't help."

"I'll wait outside," Apollo replied.

"Thank you," the winged god said.

Apollo stood outside his bedroom and waited. Desire had overtaken him when he had stumbled upon the god of love doing what he did best. That was the reaction Eros got no matter where he went. He could be covered in mud, and anyone standing next to him would become aroused and filled with love.

Apollo went outside and stared at the clouds and thought of something else besides Eros and the nymph making love so close to him. His arousal increased when he heard their passionate cries and moans as they both climaxed. A few minutes later, Eros stepped out of his home and greeted Apollo. Eros' cheeks were bright pink and his skin was glistening with a light coat of sweat. The god of love was naked and Apollo failed in his attempt to look away. He was still tempted by the beautiful god.

"Now, how can I help you?" He used the back of his hand to wipe the sweat off his forehead. Apollo wasted no time with small talk and pleasantries.

"Have you come across a young girl named Daphne?"

Eros thought about the name for what seemed like an eternity to Apollo before answering the question. "No, I don't think I've ever heard of her."

"Are you certain? She hasn't tried to approach you? You haven't seen a girl with dark green hair hiding in the bushes like some of the mortal women do when they fall in love with you?" Apollo raised a brow.

"Yes, I'm certain. No, I've never seen or heard of your Daphne."

"Then . . . Eos was wrong," Apollo whispered. He thought about the meaning behind each word in that sentence. His best friend . . . his confidante, had lied to him. Why?

"Who was wrong?"

"No one. Never mind. Thank you, Eros." He patted Eros on the shoulder and walked away.

Apollo didn't know whether he should confront his findings with Eos or go see Daphne.

What if Eos lies to me again? I don't think I could stand it.

He decided to ask Daphne himself. He felt that it would be better to discover the truth from the source.

CHAPTER 11

Just take her. That's what Hades did when he saw and fell in love with Persephone that day in the field. Just take her even if it brings chaos into the world. No, no, you fool, you can't do that. It would be wrong. Now mortals have winter because of Hades' selfish deed. The mortals will surely die if I brought yet another disruption into their world. And that won't make Daphne fall in love with me. That will only help push her further away.

Apollo was so close to Daphne he could see and smell her. Her skin held traces of river water and lilacs. His eyes took in her beauty as though he were a hungry wolf. Daphne's flesh was so pale he could see every freckle. Her hair was green like the sun rising over an oak tree. Apollo could now see that her eyes were dark olive. And her lips . . . how he yearned to kiss her luscious lips.

How long will I have to wait?

Daphne hummed to herself as she combed her long hair

with a fine gold comb while Stilbe swam in the river. A single strand of her hair fluttered through the air, curling this way and that way. He watched, mesmerized at it traveled until it reached Apollo's wrist. His heart skipped a beat when he felt the delicate strand caress his skin. He grabbed the hair and stared at it, mesmerized by how it glistened like an emerald.

If this isn't love . . . then I don't know what is.

"Did you hear that?" Daphne paused, comb mid-stroke.

"Hear what?" Stilbe popped out of the water.

Daphne looked around. "I thought I heard a man whispering. It was probably nothing."

"Maybe you're just imagining things," her sister said.

"Perhaps you're right."

Stilbe took a mouthful of water and spat it at Daphne, teasing her. "I'm a fountain."

Daphne rolled her eyes and continued combing her hair.

She heard me, he thought. *She's the one. She's the one for me.*

He took a deep breath and stepped out of his hiding place. He made sure that all of his power showed. He wanted there to be no doubts in their minds as to who he was. Daphne's eyes widened the moment her gaze fell upon him.

"Stilbe," Daphne whispered.

"What is it?" Stilbe turned, then gasped. "Oh my goodness." She quickly got out of the water and bowed before Apollo. Daphne immediately followed suit.

Good, they know who I am.

"Oh, mighty Apollo. How kind of you to grace us with your presence," Daphne said.

"You may rise," he said.

Daphne and Stilbe carefully rose to their feet, making certain that they adverted their gaze. They didn't dare look at Apollo's face. The last thing they wanted was to disrespect a god.

Apollo glanced at Stilbe; she was certainly attractive and had her own charms and grace, but she was nothing compared to Daphne.

"You know who I am?"

"Yes," Daphne replied.

Stilbe could only respond with a quick nod.

"I hope you don't mind," he said to Stilbe, "but I'm going to steal your sister away from you for a moment."

Again, Stilbe only nodded.

"Good. Daphne, will you join me for a walk?"

Daphne was speechless; for a moment she wondered what it was she had done to garner such attention from a god.

But instead of asking him, she said, "Of course."

As she walked away with Apollo, Daphne glanced at her sister one more time and noticed how her eyes flashed green with envy. She had never seen that look on her face before; Stilbe looked old and angry as though she had aged that very second. This was another reason why Daphne had vowed never to marry. The very reason why she stayed away from men in the first place. She valued her sister far too much to let a man come between them. She didn't care what it cost her, but she would do whatever it took to get the mighty sun god away from her.

"I have been watching you for the past several days," Apollo said.

"Really? I hope I haven't done anything to offend you to have garnered your attention in such a way," Daphne said.

"To be honest, I have had visions of you since I was a young boy. Your beauty has captivated me for as long as I can remember. And now . . . I have finally found you." He gave her his best smile.

Daphne smiled back and tried to pretend to be happy in his presence. She could only imagine the look on her father's face upon telling him that Apollo fancied her.

"Forgive me, Master Apollo, I am undeserving of such flattery," she said. "It is my sister Stilbe to whom you should say such lovely things."

"Why?" Surprised, he looked at Daphne once more, trying to see if perhaps she was right. What if he was wrong about her? But the more he studied her features and her actions, the more intrigued he was by her. Why would she not want his attention? Why would she want to steer him away when there were hundreds, thousands of women who would kill to stand in her place?

"Is it because of your infatuation with Eros? You can tell me, I will not be offended." His tone was harsher than he'd intended. But hadn't he just confirmed with Eros that he had never seen Daphne?

Apollo didn't sound as sweet as he had a second ago. His voice had changed as he had asked that question—it was harsh, rude, almost angry. Daphne could tell by that tone that Apollo *would* be offended if she chose to express love for Eros.

"No," she said.

"Forgive me. I was under the impression that you were." His

voice softened as he spoke. He was pleased with her reply. She was free for him to pursue.

Daphne tucked her hair behind her ear and gave him the tiniest of grins. "Forgive me for being so bold, but whoever gave you that information was greatly misinformed," she said.

"I feared as much." He nodded.

Daphne studied his features. He truly was a sight to behold; she had never gazed upon such a marvelous looking man. His skin looked as though someone had taken gold dust and rubbed it lightly against it. His brilliant blue eyes seemed to turn a different shade of the sky every time she looked into them. But a vow was a vow, and she wasn't the type of woman who would go back on something she swore, even if it was only to herself in the darkness. "Why are you here?"

"Isn't it obvious? I'm here for you." He smiled.

"You really have the wrong sister." Daphne took a deep breath.

"Why do you keep saying that?"

"Because, Master Apollo . . . I have taken a vow of celibacy, and I have no intention of ever breaking it, no matter how handsome or powerful you are," she said.

Apollo was taken aback. He couldn't believe his ears. Never in his entire life had he ever been rejected.

EROS YAWNED AND STRETCHED his body as though he were trying to touch the clouds with his fingertips. His white feather wings stretched out horizontally, his body appearing to mimic a cross.

"Hello, Eros." A female voice spoke from behind him.

"Well, well, well, if it isn't the woman who rises with the sun god," he said.

"Oh, stop." Eos' cheeks turned bright pink.

"What can I do for you?"

"Has Apollo come to you asking about Daphne?"

"Yes," he replied, finally turning around to face her.

Eos was a beauty in her own right. She could have any man—god or mortal. She could've been a daughter of Aphrodite she was so lovely to gaze upon. Why of all people did she choose Apollo? A god who was fixated on another woman.

"I'm going to have a closer look at this girl. Her name is uttered everywhere I go today," Eros muttered.

"Apollo is intrigued by her and refuses to acknowledge that I'm standing right next to him, ready and willing to be at his beck and call." Eos sounded frustrated. "I would be his everything if he would just look at me the way he looks at *her*. I wish he would realize it."

"Sounds like someone is in love," Eros teased. "I wonder if it will be anything like when you were in love with Orion."

"Stop it. Don't you dare utter his name," she warned.

"Or how about Astraios, Cephalus, Clitus, and Ganymede?"

"Silence!" she roared. Her chest rose and fell rapidly. She couldn't control the breaths coming out of her lungs.

"Happy you can see my point," he said.

Eos thought about all the lovers she'd had in the past and the children she bore for each one. Stars, planets, and the four winds were born because of Astraios' seed. She recalled the love she had felt for each of her lovers and wondered why it never worked for her. Why did all of her relationships end horribly or with someone dying? Her eyes fell on Eros and his quiver full of golden and lead-tipped arrows. Gold for love, lead for hate.

"It's your fault," she whispered.

"What?" He was unable to believe what she had said.

Eos pointed an accusatory finger at him. "It's your fault. You and your damned arrows. You made me fall in love with all those men," she said.

"That is ridiculous, you were already infatuated. All I did was push you in the right direction. Otherwise, you would still be alone and miserable," he said.

She stomped her foot and shrieked, "I am alone and miserable. Nothing has changed. You need to fix this."

Eros arched an eyebrow and crossed his arms over his chest. "And how exactly am I supposed to do that? I can't force Apollo to fall in love with you."

"True, but you can help *push him in the right direction*." Eos used his own words against him.

Could I force love, Eros thought. *Force something that was supposed to be so beautiful, pure and organic?*

"No," he whispered.

"No?"

"I can't do it. It will have terrible consequences," he said.

"Why?" she cried.

"Because even though it didn't work with you and your lovers, I still succeeded in making you fall in love. You gave birth to planets and stars. If I hadn't pushed things along for you, the sky would have nothing but the waxing and waning moon up in the heavens and, judging by how Artemis is doing, that would be a very plain sight to see."

"I would much rather have the man that puts the sun up in the sky and illuminates the world with his smile than all of the stars and planets in the sky," she said.

"You don't mean that. You love your children. I've seen the way you look at them. You can't lie to me about that, Eos, not about love."

"Please, help me, Eros. Why won't you help me?" A lump formed in her throat. Her heart ached for Apollo . . . day in and day out. The aching . . . she was tired of the one-sided love. Tears fell softly down her cheeks.

"You don't know what you're asking of me," he replied, forcing himself to look away from the beautiful crying goddess. He knew how much she suffered from lack of love. She needed it as much as mortals needed air to breathe. It was why she produced such magnificent offspring. No one but she could have given birth to the stars, planets, the four winds, and the bravest soldiers known to mankind. Gods knew what she would produce if she mated with Apollo.

What if it's wrong to tamper with such things? Especially if they are not meant to be?

HERMES COULDN'T HELP but grin. He had finally done it. He had finally put a look of utter confusion on Apollo's handsome face.

That'll show him. He giggled. *He thinks he's so much better than everyone else. I'd like to see him try to teach a five-year-old how to pick pockets. It's not as easy as it looks. There are methods to these sorts of things. He thinks all people need is sunshine and blue skies. Well they don't. They need money and food. Without these things, they may as well bake under the sun while they starve.*

Hermes had decided it was time someone played a little trick on the sun god. So he had stolen his sheep and painted them all a different color. Apollo would never be able to find them. Then Hermes had then given them to families that were struggling to survive. As one of the few gods who spent most of his time with the mortals, Hermes had always been curious of how they lived every day, knowing one day they might die unexpectedly. Gods didn't have to worry about such things. They would never know hunger, thirst, or any kind of bodily suffering. Hermes wanted to teach them more efficient ways to survive, which was why he was now teaching a five-year-old orphan how to steal a rich man's gold.

Sure, it's gold that I myself helped put inside that man's pocket in the first place, but I wasn't about to idly stand by and watch a little boy starve to death.

"You just bump into him and apologize profusely while making sure all of his clothes are nice and clean. But what you're really doing is finding out where his money is while he's flustered," Hermes whispered into the boy's ear. "When you find his gold, you wait until he turns around, ready to walk away, and you take his money. Do you understand?"

The child looked at him with large green eyes and nodded.

"Go and give it a try. I'll be right here watching," he said.

The little boy ran off toward the nicely dressed merchant and did exactly as Hermes taught him. The little boy turned to Hermes and gave him a gap-toothed smile. Hermes chuckled. He knew the boy would grow up to be a success no matter what he chose to do in life.

Hermes walked away, leaving the small town where he had held temporary residence. He was finished there. He would travel the world and see where else he was needed. There was always a thief who needed to be taught a lesson or two, a shepherdess who needed to learn how to keep her sheep close by, or a merchant who had to learn not to squander all his money on things he didn't need. Mortals assumed that he was only a messenger to the gods. He only did that in his spare time; besides, that didn't take up too much time. All the gods did was squabble and screw each other. It was one big dysfunctional family.

He walked along the path, making his way toward Athens when he overheard a deep male voice and a light feminine voice. He smiled his wicked, mischievous smile and climbed the nearest tree. As quietly as he could manage, he nestled himself on one of the branches and watched the scene playing out beneath him.

Well, well, well . . . look who it is.

Eos and Eros were discussing her disastrous love life, and she was placing most of the blame on Eros and his arrows. He suppressed the urge to laugh. Eos was the most lovesick goddess Hermes had ever met. Every time he spoke to her, she was in love with someone new. No one ever said anything to her about it because she always produced such marvelous offspring after she made love. It was as though Eos didn't have it in her to make anything less than wonderful children.

"You owe me," Eos said.

"I owe you nothing," the god of love replied.

"Yes, you do," she insisted.

Hermes wished he had arrived a few minutes sooner so he could have heard what they had already said to each other. He was certain it had something to do with her past and the men in her life. There were rumors about how Aphrodite had made Eos lovesick in order to take revenge for the part she took in the murder of Adonis. Eos was the one who had told Ares of Aphrodite's feelings for the handsome Adonis. Ares, angry that this mortal boy was getting attention from his lover, had transformed into a wild boar and gored Adonis to death while Aphrodite watched from a distance, unable to move or utter a sound in protest. Naturally, Hermes had been there because he was the one who had delivered the message.

Ares and Eos both paid the price for slaying an innocent young man, whose only crime was the admiration of the goddess of beauty and love. Ares was bound in chains and imprisoned inside a giant bronze cauldron where he remained for thirteen months until Zeus commanded Hermes to rescue him. Aphrodite made sure that Eos, who had been the troublemaker, would know for all time what it was like to love someone and not be loved in return.

"Please, Eros. Please help me," Eos pleaded. "At least get him to notice me. Help me get a genuine smile out of him. A smile just for me."

Well, I have to hand it to Aphrodite, Hermes thought, *she certainly knows how to cast a spell. It's always those who are in love who suffer the most. I'm glad I don't have to worry about any of that nonsense. It's a good thing I'm the one who gets to sleep with the mighty Aphrodite every once in a while.*

He grinned wickedly.

Eros let out a long, drawn out sigh. His golden curls bounced with no effort. Hermes could see the despair in Eros' eyes as he searched the skies for an answer.

He's trying to do the right thing, Hermes thought. *Don't do it. Stay out of it. This will get messy. You will suffer for meddling in things you won't be able to control.*

Hermes wanted to project these thoughts into Eros' mind, but he didn't want anyone to know he was eavesdropping.

"Fine," Eros whispered.

Fine. Such a dirty word. It's almost as though you're saying nothing at all.

"Thank you, thank you, thank you." Eos smiled and kissed the god of love on each cheek.

I wonder who the unlucky man is.

"Apollo and I will be so happy," she said.

Hermes had to bite his tongue to keep from bursting into laughter. He almost fell out of the tree from the shock. He couldn't believe his luck. First, he had fiddled with Apollo's flock of sheep and and now he gets to watch Eros tinker with the sun god's heart. This was a day of mischief that would never be forgotten.

CHAPTER 12

"You thought I was in love with Eros?" Daphne ventured a glance at Apollo.

"At least . . . that's what I heard." Apollo grinned.

Daphne laughed. It was the clearest, most beautiful sound Apollo had ever heard in his whole life. Her teeth were perfect white pearls all in a row. Her tongue was a moist pink hill hiding in the cave of her mouth. He could probably go on and on, finding a poem for each part of her body.

"Such a shame." He shook his head.

"Oh, dear. Sweet Master Apollo," Daphne said gently, "you will find someone who is much better suited for you."

"Well, whoever she is and wherever she may be, I certainly hope she is as charming as you," he said.

Daphne blushed.

Apollo opened, then closed his mouth. He wasn't entirely sure what her answer to this question would be. The last thing he wanted to do was offend her, but no matter how hard he tried, he couldn't form the question in his mind. The words wouldn't come out properly. So, he did what seemed natural to him; he placed his hand on the back of her head, pulled her toward him, and kissed her. Daphne let out a gasp of surprise, but she didn't fight him. She tensed for a moment and reluctantly relaxed her body. He breathed in the scent of her as he gently pushed his tongue inside of her mouth.

Daphne carefully, as gently as possible, pulled herself away from the sun god. She was amazed by how incredibly warm he felt. She didn't know why that surprised her so much. What else should she expect? He was Apollo, master of the sun, prophecy, and medicine. The only thing he could be was warm.

"Dear, sweet Apollo." Daphne placed her hand on her chest. She could feel her heart beating fast beneath her fingertips.

"Yes?"

"I still don't understand." She searched his face with her dark olive eyes for an answer. Something that would somehow be written across his face, something that could explain to her why the night after she vowed to stay celibate for the rest of her life Apollo would suddenly appear and take notice of her.

"Maybe there is nothing to understand." There it was; Apollo's heart almost burst out of his chest as he realized that this was the kiss he had seen in his vision. The vision he'd had years ago that had been haunting him for as long as he could remember. The kiss, the perfect kiss he had been yearning for his entire life. Lips upon lips. Skin against skin. And a softness that was almost unbearable. This was it. Even if they never mated. Even if all she did was go home with him and remain near him for all times, he wouldn't question her vow of celibacy. All he wanted was to be near her for the rest of his life.

Sadly, the kiss had come to an end. He took her hands and brought them close to his lips, holding on for dear life, as though she would vanish if he let her go for a second.

"Come with me. You will have anything your heart desires," he said. "I promise not to touch you unless you wish to be touched. I will promise you anything if you would just say you will come home with me."

He gently touched her face and cheeks with his fingertips. He wanted to memorize every curvature, every inch of her skin so that he might conjure up the memory of this moment whenever he desired.

Daphne smiled and blushed once more. Her eyes locked with his; she could see the love and desire emanating from his blue gaze. "Can I have a day to think about it?"

Ah, finally . . . a glimmer of hope.

"I will come for you in the morning." Apollo took her hand and planted a soft kiss on her knuckles. He smiled, then vanished.

"Oh dear," Daphne whispered. Hours after he was gone, she could still feel his kiss on her hand.

WELL, THINGS HAVE FINALLY gotten interesting around here, Hermes thought as he followed Eros to where Apollo and Daphne connected in a soul-piercing kiss.

"Shoot the arrow of hate at Apollo," Eos had told Eros. *"Make*

him hate the very sight of her. Shoot her with the arrow of love when Apollo isn't looking so she may fall in love with someone or something else other than Apollo."

Eros shook his head; he was still reluctant to interfere with Apollo's feelings for Daphne.

Hermes waited quietly for his moment.

How dare they try to understand what goes on inside the heart? Hermes thought. *Who are we to judge? Who are we to tell people what they are supposed to feel? This will remind him and Eos what happens when we tamper and meddle in things that are none of our business.*

Eros pulled out the lead arrow, placed it on his bow, and poised himself to launch it straight into Apollo's heart. Then Hermes noticed a shadow of doubt cross his face.

He's still not sure. Even after he promised Eos that he would do it, he still has doubts.

Eros put the arrow back in the quiver and vanished.

"YOU DIDN'T DO IT, DID YOU?" Eos already knew the answer Eros would give her.

"You should've seen the way he kissed her," he said, his voice full of emotion. "Like she was the whole world, the answer to everything for which he is searching for. I couldn't take that away from him. Things like that come only once in a lifetime. No matter how much you beg, I won't do it. I won't go back there and ruin their lives."

Judging by the finality in his voice, Eos knew that she would have to use every trick up her sleeve to get Eros to go along with their original plan.

"Eos, if you want, I can help you find someone who looks exactly like Apollo. Someone who can genuinely love you for who you are, for your beauty and your thoughtfulness."

As Eros spoke, Eos knew he meant every word he said. He was being sincere and kind. He was trying to do the right thing. None of that mattered, however. Every word the god of love spoke cut her like a thousand knives. How could she possibly settle for anything less than the sun god? How could she knowingly look upon another man's face while in the back of her mind wishing he were someone else? How could she live with herself? Another man wouldn't do. Even if someone gave her an exact copy of Apollo, it still wouldn't be the same, it wasn't something she would happily accept.

"I'm sorry, Eros, but there's only one man for me," she whispered.

"I'm sorry, but I'm not going to help you," he replied.

He vanished and left her alone with her thoughts and solace. Eos burst into tears as soon as he disappeared. She knew what was coming: the confrontation. Her lies. Apollo's angry face. He was always so handsome, even when he was angry. Nothing would relinquish her love for him. Even if she were to die by his hand, she would still find reason to be content that he had found *some* excuse to touch her. Oh, how she longed to feel his warm hands against her skin. Eos went back home where she cried and waited for the inevitable.

Hermes followed Eros until he stopped in a field of blue hyacinths, which Hermes found ironic since this was the very place where Apollo's last lover had died. He was amazed how the blue-violet flower matched the color of the young man's eyes. Some still weren't sure as to what exactly happened to the handsome youth, but everyone knew how Apollo had felt about Hyacinthus. The way they had looked at each other let the world know of their feelings for each other. It was as though the answer to all of their questions and worries lay inside of them. Nothing could possibly go wrong as long as they had each other. Some even went so far as to say the boy was the love of Apollo's life.

Apollo was incredibly lucky and unlucky at love. He had a knack for finding marvelous lovers, but he lost them so easily and tragically. The deeper he loved them, the worse the tragedy.

"What did you think you were going to accomplish?" Hermes sat down next to arrow-bearing god.

"What are you talking about?" Eros didn't look at Hermes.

"Why did you tell Eos that you would do it? Why did you change your mind?"

"You already know the answer to those questions. I don't know why you bother asking me." Eros shook his head.

"There's a difference between hearing something while eavesdropping and getting a direct answer to a direct question."

Eros turned his divine blue eyes to Hermes. The white of his eyes were light pink as if he'd been fighting back tears all day.

He took a deep breath and gazed at the field of flowers before he answered Hermes.

"I told Eos I would do it because I could see the pain in her heart," Eros began. "It is something that she carries with her every single day. I also saw the pure love she has for Apollo. It was white hot and blinding. How could anyone say no to that? And then I saw Apollo and Daphne in the forest. You were there, too, I could sense you. Did you see the look on his face while he was kissing her? It was as though she were the answer to every question he'd ever had in his entire life. How could I possibly take that away from him? He has suffered just as much as Eos when it comes to matters of love. At least Eos has something to show for it. Apollo has no offspring, nothing by which to remember his lovers."

"Unfortunately, for you . . ." Hermes sighed. "You did the right thing."

"Eos is upset."

"I know."

"She won't accept anyone other than Apollo. I offered to have Aphrodite create the perfect man for her. An exact replica of Apollo if that was what she desired, but she refused."

"I don't blame her for turning down the offer. I wouldn't accept it either," Hermes said.

"What do I do now?" Eros looked more like a confused young man than a god.

"That is for The Moirae to know and for us to eventually, if we're lucky, find out," Hermes replied. He reached out and grabbed a hyacinth. He had never seen such a beautiful plant before. *A flower within a flower*, he thought.

The stem was riddled with lots of tiny blue-violet blooms. He brought it close to his nose and took in the delicate scent that came from the petals. Apollo had done the right thing by not letting Hades stake his claim on young Hyacinthus. This was the only way one could truly become immortal.

You have to transform into something else. Hermes remained pensive as he studied the flower in his hand. Hermes wondered if his day would come, if he would ever have to choose between dying and becoming something else.

What will it feel like not to be myself? Will my soul be multiplied by a million or just one soul spread far too thin for the world to even notice my existence?

APOLLO LEFT DAPHNE TO think about his offer. He needed to go home and confront Eos, to ask her why she had lied to him.

She is supposed to be my most trusted friend. Why would she do such a thing? He wondered as he walked through the hallways of his palace in search of the rosy-fingered goddess. It wasn't until he heard her loud sobs that he was able to locate her sitting on the floor of the balcony.

"The sun is setting," she whispered as she touched the sky and slowly took away the pink and peach tinge that still remained up on the heavens. Even from behind, he could tell that she had had a difficult day as well. Her shoulders were slumped; she looked like Atlas, forever carrying the world on his back.

"Hello, Apollo." She didn't turn to face him.

"Hello, Eos," he replied.

She sighed at his voice saying her name.

"I heard you finally spoke to Daphne." She wiped a runaway tear from her cheek.

"I did. She told me some interesting things. Things that made me wonder about you," he said.

Eos turned around and threw herself at his feet.

Ah . . . so she is guilty.

"Apollo, please forgive me," she begged as she touched his feet with her forehead.

He could feel her hot tears splash against his toes. *Liar*, he thought as each tear stung his skin.

"Get up," he snapped.

Eos quickly scrambled to her feet and did the best she could to compose herself. She wiped the tears that continuously fell from her eyes and tucked her black hair behind her ears.

"You lied to me," he whispered. "Knowing how I despise liars, you did it anyway. You know that I see everything eventually. There is nothing that can be hidden from me. Even if your plan had succeeded, it still would've been worse for you the moment I learned the truth."

"I did it for you." She reached out to touch him.

"Liar!" he roared.

She gasped, pulling her hands away as though she had been slapped.

"You are a liar." He pointed at her chest.

May as well shoot a thousand arrows at my chest, she thought, staring at his accusatory finger.

"No," she said as she shook her head.

"You told me that Daphne was infatuated with Eros." As he spoke, he moved closer to her.

The closer Apollo got, the more she inched away from him, until finally her back touched the wall and she had nowhere to hide or run.

"What were you planning on doing next? Hmm?" His voice was harsh.

Eos bit her bottom lip and trembled.

"Answer me!" He drove his fist through the wall.

Eos screamed and once more, she lied, "Nothing. I wasn't going to do anything else. I just wanted you to love me." She sobbed.

Apollo pulled his fist out of the hole he had created and shook the debris off his skin.

"Eos, I did love you," he said, his voice finally softening toward her. "But, like a sister. You and I will never *be*."

There was a finality to his words. The way he spoke them, it was as though a new law in nature had been written.

"No." Eos shook her head.

"I want you to leave," Apollo said.

"Please, no. Don't do this," she pleaded.

"I can't even look at you." He turned his face away from hers and stared at the darkening sky instead.

"Let me stay. I will make it up to you. I swear I'll stay out of your way. You won't even know I'm here," Eos pleaded. She searched for a glimmer of hope, but Apollo wouldn't meet her gaze. He ignored her and continued to search the sky for something that couldn't be found on her face.

Apollo couldn't stand the sound of her voice anymore. The more she spoke, the more he wanted to strangle her.

"Please let me stay," she tried once more.

"Enough!" he screamed. His hair burst into bright yellow and orange flames, his eyes turning red like the inside of a volcano. The Sun God personified. A man made of molten lava.

"Eos," he said, "if you don't leave my home this very second, Hades will have to dig up your remains at the bottom of the River Styx. I swear on the River Styx that I will do it. Do not test my patience, Eos. You have toyed with me enough for one day."

Eos stared at Apollo's new form. She had never seen him so angry, and despite his anger, she was drawn to him like a moth to a flame. All she wanted to do was push her fingers into him and get burned. But she knew better. She ran away, leaving a trail of tears behind her. Her tiny sandaled feet slapped against the marble floor until there was only silence.

After several moments the fire and lava vanished from his body. It took him a while before he could breathe normally again. Even though he was still livid with Eos, he did feel a twinge of sorrow for the way he had spoken to her. He shook his head, remembering why she needed to leave and decided against calling her back to give her one last chance. It was for the best they part ways.

She shouldn't have lied to me. If she truly loved me, she wouldn't have done such a thing.

CHAPTER 13

Artemis sensed her brother's anger and rage. She watched as every major volcano around the world erupted, spilling red hot lava, causing chaos and mayhem. She enlisted Poseidon's help, asking him to create tsunamis large enough to go inland, cooling some of the lava that had flowed toward the towns.

She could feel Apollo's heart beating against her chest at a strange pace. She was happy to have such a close connection with her brother. It felt like there was an invisible line that connected them to each other; she always knew when he needed her even if they were miles apart.

Artemis closed her eyes and willed herself to Apollo's palace. When she opened her eyes, she found herself in the middle of his glorious garden. The flowers used to change according to his moods, and today every single bloom in the garden was a white orchid. For a long time the flowers in this garden held only hyacinths. It was a welcome alteration.

She finally found her brother. "Are you all right?"

He was lying down underneath a maple tree, holding one of the orchids in his hands. He stared at it as though somewhere on its soft white petals lie the answer to his problems.

"Shhh." He pressed his index finger to his lips. "Don't ruin the moment with talk."

"An hour before I decided to come here, several volcanoes throughout the world erupted. I was wondering if you had anything to do with that, little brother." Artemis glared at Apollo.

"Leave me alone," he said.

"Many people lost their lives today, and that's all you have to say?"

"The Moirae are the ones in control of the fates of people. Not I," Apollo replied.

"What happened?" Artemis demanded.

"Eos happened."

"What about her?"

"She lied to me."

Artemis' eyebrows rose in surprise. She knew that lying to Apollo was the worst possible thing you could do to him. That or to call *him* a liar, as she had done many times as a child, enduring his wrath.

"Eos?"

"Yes."

"I didn't know she was capable of such a thing," Artemis said.

"Neither did I," Apollo said.

"What did she lie about?"

"About a girl."

Artemis snorted and rolled her eyes. "Is that all?"

"A very special girl. The one from my visions," he explained as he took the white orchid and gently caressed it with his fingertips.

"Really? She's real? An actual person who lives in a realm outside of your head?" Artemis tried not to laugh.

"I'm serious," Apollo said.

"So am I," Artemis replied. "Is she in love with you?"

"Who?"

"Eos."

"Oh, *her*." His handsome face wrinkled at the thought of the goddess of dawn. "That's what she said anyway."

"Lovesick whore," Artemis spat.

"Don't call her that," he said.

"What else should I call her?"

"I don't know. I think I'd prefer it if you didn't mention her name altogether." Apollo pinched the bridge of his nose as he tried to think of something other than the defeated look on Eos' face.

"So . . . please explain to me why every flower in your garden is an orchid." Artemis plucked one of the exotic blooms and studied the delicate white petals.

"This flower is called Phalaenopsis, if you must know," he explained, "and I've changed them because they are Daphne's favorite flower."

"Who is Daphne?"

He let out a happy sigh as he thought of Daphne. "She is the most radiant and charming being in all the world," he said.

"Don't you ever get tired of falling in love every few months?"

"Is your heart so cold that you have not found someone to warm your bed at night?" he retorted.

"Unlike you, brother, I have no need for such diversions. I have better things to do with my time," Artemis said.

"Artemis, there is nothing wrong with finding a companion. Nothing sexual has to happen if you don't want it to. You can kiss, and nothing else has to come of it, but you must get that archaic thought of Mother and Father out of your head. He didn't rape her. He didn't force her to do anything she didn't want to do." Apollo grumbled and added, "That he seduced her and forgot about her for a while is a completely different story."

"You're disgusting," Artemis said, her delicate features wrinkling.

"And you, my virgin sister, are not disgusting enough. You should try to get your hands dirty every once in a while," he teased.

"Besides, even if I *were* interested in finding someone, that person doesn't exist. Not in this world or the next." Artemis' voice grew sad and distant as she thought of all the cold and lonely nights she had spent in her life. Apollo noticed his sister's distress.

"I'm sorry, sister. I didn't mean to make you sad." Apollo stood and embraced his twin. "I was only teasing you. I didn't know this was a really serious matter for you."

"It's all right, Apollo. I've grown accustomed to seeing my own shadow walking in front of me. My hounds are company enough for me."

Apollo rested his head on Artemis' shoulder and said, "I sometimes wish I was Eros. I would help you find love with gold-tipped arrows and let love bloom inside of you for the world to see. You know something?"

"What?"

"I haven't seen you smile in a long time, sister. Why is that?"

Artemis sighed and stared off into space. She wasn't sure she wanted to answer that question. She often felt it was best to keep things to herself, but she found it in her heart to speak. "I have been bored with life since the day I was born," she began. "We are not all made to shimmer and glimmer under the sunlight, my dear brother. Not all smiles are as wide as yours. Sometimes, I wish I had never been born. I have nothing that keeps me anchored to this world. The only thing that keeps me from throwing myself into the middle of a volcano is you and mother. Besides, I wouldn't want to spend the rest of my days like a piece of black charcoal, especially since gods can't die."

"Shh." Apollo touched his sister's lips with his fingertips. "Don't say such things." He looked at Artemis as though he were seeing her for the first time.

"I'm sorry." Artemis sniffed, trying to fight the urge to cry.

"How would I have been able to exist without you by my side?" Apollo whispered. "You and I are cut from the same cloth, straight down the middle. If anything ever happened to you, I may as well vanish since you would've taken half of me down to the Underworld with you."

"I have nothing to smile for, little brother."

"Then we shall have to find something for you that will make life worth living," Apollo said with fierce determination.

"Good luck." Artemis kissed her brother on the forehead.

Eos was staring off into space. All she wanted to do was throw herself into the ocean and let her body sink to the bottom.

"Perhaps Poseidon will give me a proper burial out of pity," she whispered.

Eos continued to gaze at the horizon. Apollo would soon rise for the first time in half a century without her by his side. She closed her eyes and imagined herself beside him, watching his chest's rhythmic rise and fall, his blonde hair glinting across his forehead. The way his blue eyes would flutter open like butterfly wings. How would she ever be able to survive without him? How would she be able to break from a routine that had been with her for the past fifty years?

Eros had heard her voice and followed it until he found her alone by the edge of a cliff.

What is she doing?

He called her name several times as he ran up to her, but she didn't respond. She continued to mutter.

"I will be one with the sun." She breathed the words softly into the world as though she were sharing a secret she should've kept to herself.

Eros didn't know what she was talking about until he saw her burst into golden-orange flames.

"No!" he shouted as he reached out to her and tried to hold on to her physical body. He was amazed that the flames didn't burn him.

"Eos, please . . . don't do this," he said as he held her shoulders.

"I will be one with the sun," she repeated and then gave him a smile. She knew Apollo would mount his chariot soon. She would be there to welcome the sun into the world. No matter what happened she would always be the announcer, she would be the one to tell the world that the sun would rise.

A sigh escaped her lips, and her body, still in flames, floated up to the sky as the sun broke through the horizon.

"Oh, Eos," Eros said, gazing at the sky. He had never seen a more glorious sunrise. The sky was tinged pink, peach, and red. The rosy-fingered goddess was no more, but had become something greater. Even now, he could still hear her sigh as the sun rose higher and higher across the heavens.

The gods knew that Eros didn't love her, but that was no way for a beautiful woman to leave the world. As the sky changed from the deep blush to a cool blue, he knew what he was going to do next.

"My arrows will sing your name as they dance through the air, and I will aim straight for Apollo's heart." He vowed.

"Have you thought about Apollo's offer?" Stilbe was braiding Daphne's long, hunter green hair.

"Yes, and even that seems wrong," she replied.

"Why?"

"Because I made a promise," Daphne answered. "Even if it was only to myself, it still meant something to me. What good is a person if she cannot keep her word? What type of person would I be if people couldn't trust in the things I say?"

"Who cares? The Sun god has taken quite a liking to you. Enjoy the moment. Bask in it, he may be the only man that ever looks at you that way . . . ever," Stilbe teased.

"Oh, shush, you. What good are you to me anyway? Between you and father, the two of you would be perfectly content to marry me off to a wayward merchant if it would only give father a grandchild." Daphne tried hard not to smile. She liked talking to her sister this way. It made her remember when they were young girls together and didn't have to worry about men or getting married or anything that became too complicated. They were just sisters. Just Daphne and Stilbe, always playing. Always laughing.

Those days are over now. We can never go back to those days filled with nothing but joy, when life was simple.

"Are you all right? You look like your mind is elsewhere." Stilbe finished braiding Daphne's hair and used a white ribbon to tie the end of her locks.

"Do you ever wish things had never changed? That we could have stayed children for a longer period of time?" Daphne gazed at her sister.

Stilbe thought about the question for a moment. "No. I don't miss being a child, Daphne. I'm sorry, I never got used to being so small and unable to do anything because of it. Yes, it was nice playing and not having anything to worry about, but life isn't like that. We change, we grow, we are like water. We flow toward something greater than ourselves. We were never made to stand still and let the world pass us by. I intend to flow like the river, always toward the ocean, always toward something different."

Daphne took a deep breath and knew that this would be the last time she would speak to her sister about such things.

"She won't go with you," Artemis said.

"Don't say that," Apollo replied.

"She made a vow of celibacy. If she has any honor at all, she won't go with you. Think about it. What sort of woman will she become if she were to stay with you? How long will she remain untouched before you give in to temptation? What will you do with yourself if you can't contain your *passion* or your so-called love for her?"

"Leave me alone. Why must you ruin everything for me?"

"You need to face reality, little brother. Just because you have domain over the light doesn't mean that you see everything clearer than I do," she said.

"Please, leave me alone." He moaned.

"You have to think things through, Apollo. It's all right to listen to your heart, but what good is it if you don't listen to your mind as well?" She tapped the side of his head.

He brushed her hand aside. "And when are you going to listen to your heart a little more? Don't let it wither and die with the rest of you."

"I'm leaving." Artemis threw her hands up in the air. She didn't know why she bothered trying to convince him to do otherwise. He was as stubborn as she. They were both cut from the same exact cloth, he was right about that, but the more she looked at him, the harder it was for her to believe that they were ever inside the same womb.

"Sometimes . . . sometimes I swear I don't even know who you are," Artemis mumbled trying to hide the tears that threatened to fall down her cheeks. And with that, she finally left Apollo's palace.

Apollo didn't know how to react to his sister's words. He had never heard her speak in such a way, especially to him. He always thought she was only interested in hunting and running. He wasn't aware that she was taking more pleasure out of standing still and exploring the world at a slower pace.

Maybe I'm the one who's stayed the same; whereas, she has grown, Apollo mused. *Maybe it's far too late for me to catch up to her.* He shook his head at the negative thoughts. *She's my twin. No matter what happens, we are connected by a cord not even The Moirae can cut.*

"FOOL! MAY THE GODS DAMN him for being such a stupid fool," Artemis muttered as she climbed down the mountain. "Apollo's folly and carelessness have set things in motion that will never be undone."

Artemis tied her raven black hair into a loose bun and broke into a run. She could run around the world for all eternity and never break a sweat. She wanted to get away from the world, from the sadness that plagued her, and the loneliness that threatened to take over her heart. She and Apollo hadn't had anything in common since they became gods. She often mourned the loss of her best friend. Her father was the one responsible for the rift that separated the twins. Now they were opposites for all eternity.

But no matter how much she ran or how fast her limbs moved, she still couldn't shake the feeling that something was going to happen today. She didn't want to be there to see it. She didn't want to see the look of despair on her brother's face. And even though she felt a certain animosity toward Zeus, she prayed to him for the sake of Apollo.

Not again. Please, Father, don't let him suffer the loss of love all over again. Artemis didn't know if he heard her or not. He never replied. The only thing she heard was the sound of the silky wind singing past her ear.

HERMES WATCHED AS ARTEMIS ran down the mountain. The only reason he knew it was her was because she zoomed right past him without a word. She was never one for niceties and small talk. Hermes liked small talk. He found a strange fascination with having short conversations with random people, which was why he was the perfect messenger.

Never give more than you should . . . even when you know the whole story. Only give the people what they want to hear. It's amazing the amount of information I can retain . . . things that could change the lives of the gods themselves.

Hermes chuckled and thought about Artemis once more.

"Where is she off to in such a rush?" He wondered.

She had left a trail of burnt soil behind her. He followed the trail with his gaze, and saw that it led to Apollo's palace.

"The wheels have been set in motion," he said, "and no one can undo what will be done. Not the gods, not Zeus, not even The Moirae."

PAN GIGGLED AS HE WATCHED a little boy trip on an overgrown tree root and fall flat on his face. He pointed at the child and made fun of the boy.

"You won't grow many plants inside your dirty mouth, little boy," he said.

Pan slapped his own knees several times and tried very hard not to collapse on the floor from laughing so hard. The child spat out a mouthful of leaves and brown soil. He ran away crying and wailing.

"Well . . . he wasn't any fun at all," Pan complained as he watched the only source of amusement he had found all day run off.

"Bored. I'm bored, bored, bored," he whined.

Then he felt something crawling in his curly dark blonde hair. He licked his lips and grinned.

A tasty snack . . . just for me.

As quick as lightning, Pan snatched the unlucky beetle that was sneaking around his hair and crushed it between his index finger and thumb. He popped the creature into his mouth and giggled as he crunched it.

"Delicious," he said.

Pan then heard the sound of leaves crackling and branches breaking. He tensed up, half expecting something or someone to leap out of the shadows and attack him.

"Now . . . what could that be?" he whispered, grinning wickedly.

He followed the sound until he found a dark-haired nymph sitting by the river kicking her feet in the water. She appeared to be waiting for someone. Pan couldn't help but marvel at the color of her hair. It was as though someone had taken dark emeralds and spun each stone into gorgeous locks to put on this woman's head. Her skin was pale, like ivory. But all Pan wanted to know was if her skin was as soft as it appeared.

"For whom could she be waiting?" he whispered.

He laid down on his stomach and watched her. The more he stared at her, the more he fell in love with her. He marveled over every movement she made, whether it was by her own will or the wind that twirled her hair between its invisible fingers. Butterflies flocked to her and landed on her emerald tresses, thinking they were leaves. An array of colors decorated her hair as blood orange, bone white, and cerulean butterflies softly fluttered their wings open and shut.

Pan was entranced with Daphne, but the spell was broken with the sudden appearance of Apollo. Pan sat up and scrunched up his face.

Why does he always get the beauties? Pan puzzled, still unable to believe that the nymph was with Apollo.

Out of the corner of his eye, he saw a pair of perfectly white wings. Pan was naturally curious about the unfolding events. If he couldn't have the lovely nymph, he decided that he would cause a little mischief. He sneaked up behind Eros. The gold arrows were on the right, and the lead-tipped arrows were on the left. He ran his tongue against his tiny square teeth as a wicked idea popped into his head. He suppressed the urge to giggle as he sneaked behind Eros. As quietly as he could possibly manage, he switched the position of the arrows. He backed away from the god of love and watched his misbehavior unfold.

CHAPTER 14

NOW NO ONE WILL KNOW HER. NO ONE WILL EVER KNOW who she was or what she gave to the world," Eros muttered as he grabbed an arrow and shot it straight at Apollo and quickly grabbed another one without looking and aimed it at Daphne. It wasn't until he released that final arrow that he realized something was amiss.

"No." He gasped. "It's impossible." He had pulled an arrow from the left and one from the right. They were in the wrong side of the quiver.

He saw love bloom on Apollo's face. He looked even more love struck than normal; whereas, Daphne's face hardened as it harbored nothing but hatred for the sun god.

"This is all wrong. This wasn't what she wanted. It was supposed to be the other way around," Eros muttered, remembering Eos' request.

A loud, high pitch cackle came from behind. He spun around and found Pan rolling on the ground, kicking his hooves in the air, looking very satisfied with himself. He pointed at Eros and continued to laugh.

"You should've . . ." Pan took a deep breath. His face turned red from laughing so hard. "You should've seen the look on your face."

"That wasn't supposed to happen," Eros shouted, grabbing Pan and shaking him.

"Hey, watch the fur. I go through a lot of trouble to make it look unkempt," Pan complained.

Eros growled and pushed the god of nature away from him as though his skin was covered with puss-filled warts. Pan landed on the ground. As he studied Eros' face, he realized his joke was no longer funny.

Eros took off with the goal of trying to undo what he had done.

APOLLO FELT THE STING of an arrow.

"Ah!" He hissed as he clutched his chest.

The discomfort quickly left him, and he felt his entire body becoming warmer by the second. His mind was disoriented. His vision blurred, and the only thing he could clearly see was Daphne. Somehow, the love he had for her magnified tenfold. She stood before him in a short toga that reached the knees, her arms bare, and her hunter green hair in a simple braid.

What would she look like if she were properly dressed with her hair nicely arranged? He wondered.

Daphne too felt the sting of an arrow. She was confused as to why she was there with Apollo in the first place. She had been seconds away from saying "yes" to his offer, but the reply died in her mouth. Her body felt cold as she studied his face. When he opened his mouth to speak, all she heard were shrieks that would've made banshees run away in terror.

"Beautiful, Daphne, please say you'll come and be with me for all time," he said.

"No. Leave me alone," she replied.

"Don't fear. I am the Lord of Delphi, and I love you."

"I hate you." Daphne hissed.

"Why do you say such things? Can't you see that I would do anything for you?" The pain was obvious to see on his handsome face.

"You will ruin everything. Everything you touch dies. And I won't let you touch me, not ever. I am going to be free and celibate like Artemis."

"Oh, my love, the things you say. Don't you know you and I are meant to be together?" He reached out to touch her, but she recoiled as if his hands were misshapen claws.

She took a few steps back and broke into a run.

"Please, stay with me." Apollo followed the fleeing beauty.

"Leave me alone!" Daphne shouted, continuing to run.

Apollo quickly caught up to her and whispered sweet poems into her ear. She growled in response, grunted in frustration and forced her legs to run faster.

May that never be mine.

To war with a god-lover is not war,
It is despair.

The last three lines of a poem Daphne heard long ago came to her mind. Now she knew why she had obligated herself to stay away from men. It was anguish. The fear of the unknown. The running. Always trying to be swift, cunning, and smart. She could feel her limbs growing weary. Her lungs burned from exhaustion, and she didn't know how much longer she could keep up her pace.

Just a little longer. I can almost see Father's river. I'll be safe there. I'll be safe, and Apollo will leave me alone, and this whole experience will seem like a bad dream.

Apollo couldn't understand why she was running from him. All he wanted to do was love her and kiss her for the rest of his life. Was he not kind? Was he not gentle? Was he not handsome? He was confused still as to why he chased her so ardently. He hadn't felt so passionately about her before he came to see her. Or had he? Even as all of these thoughts entered his mind, he still refused to slow his pace.

As Daphne ran, her toga fell from her body. Apollo slowed down enough to watch her naked body in motion. He grabbed the dress and continued with his pursuit, even more determined than ever to catch the beautiful Daphne.

I suffer a malady that no balm can cure, he thought.

"Father! Help me! Open the ground and let it swallow me whole. Change my form, let me be a hideous creature, anything I don't care," Daphne cried when she saw the river growing closer and closer with every step she took as Apollo gained upon her rapidly. "Just don't let him catch me."

I cannot undo what has been done, my child, but I can change you into something else, Peneus whispered into her mind.

"Do it, I don't care. Just keep me away from him. Keep me safe, for all time," she pleaded.

Very well, he replied sadly.

Daphne came to a sudden stop. She stumbled to the ground and forced herself to stand up. She tried to run once more but her body grew stiff. Her chest rose and fell rapidly as she struggled to breathe. She could feel her heart beating against her chest as though it was trying to burst out from behind her ribcage. "Father? What have you done?" Her voice slowly died on her lips.

"What is this?" Apollo asked, horrified by the scene playing out before him.

Daphne's feet turned dark brown and sank into the ground, rooting themselves to the spot. Her braid undid itself, spinning into tiny branches and quickly became covered in leaves that matched the color of her dark green hair.

"No," Apollo whispered as he witnessed the transformation. He reached out to hold her hand before she was completely lost to him, but even that was taken from him. Her once soft, pale hands became long, thick brown branches.

"No, no, no." Apollo moaned.

Eros arrived, his mouth agape as he witnessed Daphne's transformation.

"Gods help us both," the winged god whispered.

Daphne cried out as she felt her face harden. Her olive eyes searched desperately for an answer that would never come. Her gaze fell upon Apollo's, and she wondered if she had been foolish to run away from him with such haste.

It was too late for regrets or second thoughts. She knew she would never be able to swim in the river with her sister. She would never see her father again. Nor would she feel the wind caress her naked skin.

"I'm sorry," she whimpered.

"Daphne, it's all right, beautiful one, I will do what I can to undo this." Apollo watched her face turn brown as the bark slowly encased it.

She parted her lips to speak, but the transformation was complete before she was able to utter another sound.

"What is it? Speak to me," he begged. "This isn't right." Apollo frowned as his head slowly began to clear. "It wasn't supposed to happen this way. She was going to say 'yes.' I could feel the word forming on her pink lips before something happened. A sting on both our chests made the words feel all wrong. She was going to come with me, I know it." Apollo touched the dark brown bark that had just been Daphne's muscular limbs.

The tree shook as it felt Apollo's warm hands.

"Is she still in there?" Apollo stared at Eros with large hopeful eyes.

"I don't know," Eros stammered.

"Daphne? Daphne can you hear me?" Apollo cried.

Once more, the tree shook in response.

"Maybe there is still hope," Apollo said. "Perhaps I can fix this."

As soon as he spoke those words, the tree shook violently as though it were trying to scream the word "NO" at the top of its lungs.

"Father!" Apollo cried. Before he could shout out his father's name once more, Apollo appeared in the throne room at Mount Olympus. The last time he had been in this room, was when he had been given the sacred ambrosia that had turned him into a god.

How time changes everything, he thought.

Apollo found his father sitting on his throne and waiting for him to speak. He had never before seen Zeus so serious.

"Help me," Apollo pleaded. He didn't bother trying to explain the situation. He was well aware that his father had seen everything that had happened to Daphne.

"I cannot undo this ghastly deed," he explained, his voice low and grave.

"Are you not all powerful, that you cannot help your son and his love? Can you not change a tree back into a woman?" Apollo challenged his father. He hoped to instigate some type of action out of the mighty Zeus.

"I am going to pretend you didn't say that. I understand you are upset, but be certain from this point on" —Zeus suppressed his boiling rage— "to choose your words wisely."

"Why can't you change her back?" Apollo demanded.

"Because she doesn't want to be changed back."

"What? That's not possible, why would she want to remain a tree?"

"Not everyone is made for this life, my son." Zeus sighed.

"How do you know this? How could you possibly know what Daphne wants?"

"I know because she told me," Zeus replied, his grey eyes shimmered as he finally broke into a smile.

"She has no voice with which to speak." Apollo scoffed.

"Foolish boy, I hear everything. The rivers, the rocks, the sand, the wind . . . everything has a voice. You just have to stand still long enough to listen."

Zeus tapped on the side of his head as he tried to get his son to understand what he was saying. "For all of your good qualities, that has always been the one thing you lacked. You don't *listen*. You have the gift of prophecy, and you still couldn't see your own future. Are you deaf as well as blind? Your Daphne speaks to me now just as I am talking to you because I am everything. I am everywhere all at once.

"There is very little that is kept from me. The spell of hate has been broken, and even though she truly was going to run off with you, she is much more at peace now. She is happier standing still. Forever untouched by man. Forever in repose. The Moirae will never have to cut her cord because she will live on forever. Your Daphne is eternal just as you and I are immortal. As long as you remember the story of transformation that sprung out of your love, she will live on."

"That's not what I wanted," Apollo muttered.

"Did you ever once ask what *she* wanted? You are a good man, but narrow-minded and selfish at times. Perhaps your mother was right. Maybe I gave you and your sister far too much. You need to learn the value of life and, honestly, this is the best way for you to learn."

"So that's it? You won't help me?" Apollo's eyes widened.

Zeus shook his head and spread his arms showing Apollo the empty room. "There is no one to help. She doesn't want to be a woman anymore. If she ever changes her mind, believe me, I will be the first one to come to her aide. In the meantime, she remains just as she is."

"I don't understand. How did this happen?" Apollo wondered, shaking his head in disbelief. "Someone meddled. Someone intervened in our blossoming love, and I will find out who it was."

"You will find out soon enough," Zeus said. "In the meantime, think about your actions and what they cost you. Maybe you'll be wiser next time around."

APOLLO RETURNED TO DAPHNE in her new form. He slept at her feet. In the morning, he whispered all of his hopes and fears to her. He described his palace to her and the room he had chosen for her.

"I even changed all of the flowers in my garden for you. That white orchid you like, what was it called?" He frowned. "Phalaenopsis! That's it. That's the name of your orchid. I thought it was what you needed to be happy."

Daphne swayed her branches in response, as though she was saying, *I understand your grief and your pain.*

Apollo kissed the laurel tree and wished Daphne was real again. He wanted nothing more than to kiss her soft-as-rose-petal lips once more. He wanted to touch her pale skin.

"I miss you," he whispered.

Daphne remained still.

"You don't miss me?" Apollo was surprised at her motionless form.

Her branches swayed from side to side as though asking for forgiveness.

"There is no need to apologize," he said. "I know this isn't what you wanted, and I am so sorry. It's all my fault."

He climbed up the tree and sat on the branches. He lay back and stared at the leaves that were the same hunter green as Daphne's hair. The bright blue sky lay just beyond those perfect leaves. He sat there and did nothing for the longest time until he heard the crunch of dry leaves.

"Who goes there? Leave this very moment. I prefer not to be bothered," Apollo shouted.

"So, I was right after all." Artemis emerged from the shadows.

"Leave me alone." He groaned.

"You just couldn't leave her alone, could you?"

"I loved her," Apollo explained.

"And look at what your love has done to her," Artemis whispered. "Look at what it has cost you. Is this what you want for me? This type of sadness and despair? Because if this is what love is, then I would much rather be without it."

"You've got it all wrong, sister," Apollo said, finally climbing down from the comfort of Daphne's branches.

"Do I? Because from what I can tell, you have been sleeping on this tree for the past three days. The sun has been in a strange cycle since then. Although no damage has been done, you need to get over this quick, little brother, or people will die."

"Why don't you ride my chariot for a while? You've done it before," he said.

"That was because you wanted me to ride along with you."

Apollo opened and closed his mouth several times, looking more like a fish out of water than a god.

"Why must we always argue?" He balled his hands into fists.

"Because you are still acting like a foolish teenager who has fantasies about love, and that's not the way the world works. Not everyone finds someone and gets to live happily ever after. You need to wake up and learn to cope with change; otherwise, you won't last very long."

Apollo groaned and rolled his eyes. Even though he knew his sister was right, he didn't want to admit it. "Leave me alone," he said. "Please let me mourn."

"*Leave me alone*," she mimicked. "Leaving you alone is what we have all done, and look at how you have turned out. Open your eyes. Daphne would rather be a tree than be with you."

"She was going to say 'yes.' Daphne was going to come with me. I know it," Apollo insisted.

"Then what happened?"

"I don't know," he growled in frustration. That was what confused him so much. Everything was going as planned. For the first time in years, he would've been happy—truly, genuinely content—and now he would never know that joy. He looked at his sister and noticed she looked more disheveled than normal. "Where the hell have you been?"

Her dress was ripped and dirty; it looked as though she had spent the past week rolling in the dirt.

Artemis gave him a wicked smile; one he had not seen since they were children. Before they had been turned into gods. She spread her arms wide and threw her head back, basking in the sun for a moment. Her raven black hair was knotted and matted. Her toga was dirty and torn. But her cheeks were bright pink and her blue eyes glimmered with joy and knowledge. "I've been everywhere, little brother," she replied. "I have seen the world."

"What have you seen?" Apollo raised a brow curiously.

"I have seen the Great Wall in Asia. I saw the vast desert in Africa that goes on and on for what seems to be an eternity only to abruptly end at the ocean. The great pyramids. Lands that have yet to be touched by mortal men. I have been to the bottom of the sea and seen creatures that even Poseidon isn't sure how they came to be. I even went to see Hades in his kingdom underground and was allowed to pet Cerberus."

Apollo was mesmerized by the things Artemis described. He knew these things existed only because other people had told him they are real. He was always too busy to actually take the time to explore the world the way he should have from the very beginning.

He couldn't help but be jealous of his sister for so many reasons. For guarding her heart with the ferocity of a lioness. For wanting to rediscover the world and all its beauty. For not letting every tiny problem threaten to swallow her whole. Apollo still had so much to learn, and he knew it.

"You are as wise as Athena, sister . . . even though you are filthy and smell like a stag's ass." Apollo laughed at the comparison.

Artemis looked at her brother and smiled. They held each other, and without words, they knew they would be all right as long as they had each other.

Hours after Artemis left, Apollo had another visitor.

"Who goes there?" he called out.

"It is I, Eros. I wish to speak with you," he said.

Apollo glanced down. He groaned inwardly. Eros was the last person he wanted to see at the moment. The god of love would only serve to remind him of what he had lost. "Go away. I already had one visitor today. I don't want to see anyone else."

"Please, it is urgent," Eros said.

"Did you not hear what I said?" Apollo left the comfort of his hiding place in Daphne's leaves and landed on the ground with a heavy thud. He shouted, "I want to be alone."

"I have something to say that will finally explain everything that has transpired here over the past few weeks. Isn't that what you want? To understand why this happened?" Eros pointed to the tree that Daphne had become.

Apollo narrowed his eyes and glared at the winged love god. "What are you saying?"

"We should speak somewhere else," he suggested.

"Why?"

"Because what I have to say might anger you and, from what I've heard about you, your anger might set Daphne on fire." Eros pointed at the laurel tree.

Apollo, although still suspicious over Eros' intentions, conceded and went with him. They walked together side by side in silence until feeling they were at a safe distance.

"Speak," Apollo said.

"Eos is gone," he said.

Apollo flinched when he heard Eos' name. The past days without her presence had been strange for him and Eros had reminded him of her absence.

"What? That's impossible, where could she possibly have gone? Do you wish for me to go find her? Is that it?" Apollo wondered.

"You misunderstood what I said. I mean that Eos is no longer with us in this world. She is gone. Not dead because I can feel her presence still floating in and out of our realm, but her physical body no longer exists," Eros said.

Apollo couldn't believe what he had heard. He shook his head as he remembered the last time they spoke. He had hurt her beyond repair. Now he would never be able to apologize and make it up to her. His heart was heavy with guilt.

"I shouldn't have spoken to her so harshly. Damn me and my stupid mouth." He muttered and ran his fingers through his hair.

"That's not all," Eros said.

"Please" —Apollo gave him a fake smile— "tell me how else you can make this day any worse than it is already."

"You are aware that Eos lied to you about your fair Daphne," Eros said.

Apollo nodded.

Eros took a deep breath and licked his lips before he continued with his explanation. "In her despair over the thought of losing you to another, she came to me and asked me intervene with your affections for Daphne."

The sun god glared at Eros, his blue eyes seemingly glowing red. "And?"

"At first, I refused," Eros explained.

Apollo narrowed his eyes as he clenched his fists. Puffs of

smoke escaped from his hands. "At first? So you're saying there was a second offense?"

"It was a mistake," Eros said.

"You interfered with love. You are supposed to be the protector of love blossoming between two beings. You are supposed to help people fall in love, so tell me winged god, how did you interfere with my affairs?"

Eros flapped his wings nervously as he took a step back from the sun god. "It was Eos' wish for me to strike your heart with the arrow of hate so that you would forget your infatuation with Daphne and, out of pity for Daphne's loss, I was supposed to shoot her with the arrow of love so that she might find a suitor after losing you. But it didn't work out as planned."

"*Didn't work out as planned?*" Apollo echoed Eros' last words, raising his voice.

"Someone switched my arrows as I was about to shoot them."

"So that makes it all right then? That it was an accident? Not entirely your fault? You still shot the arrows at my heart and struck Daphne's as well. You should've stayed out of it. It didn't concern you. Nor did it concern Eos, that damned meddler. May she rot wherever she may be. As for you . . ." Apollo pointed at Eros' chest, wishing to do nothing but burn a hole right through his perfect chest. "Because of you, I have nothing. First, I lost Hyacinthus and now Daphne. I have lost them both forever. One year apart from each other. How will I ever be able to find two such perfect beings once more? Tell me that, god of love. Tell me where I can find a man with indigo eyes? Where can I find another woman with hunter green hair and skin as pale as milk?

A woman with charm and grace that can be compared to that of your mother Aphrodite? Where?"

"I'm sorry. I cannot help you, Apollo," Eros said. He was surprised. He half expected Apollo to set his wings on fire or at least be more upset about the whole situation by now.

Apollo's anger vanished in a puff of smoke. He was tired of feeling enraged. He was too tired . . . far too heartbroken over the loss of Daphne. He knew she would have asked him to forgive his friend. So that was what he would do. Mourn her loss in peace and learn from this harsh lesson.

"Leave me alone," Apollo said.

"Apollo, I really am sorry about everything," Eros said.

"Unless you can bring either Hyacinthus or Daphne back to me, I have nothing else to say to you, Eros."

Eros sighed. He couldn't think of anything to say to the sun god so he exhaled and flew away. Apollo watched Eros fly away until he was nothing but a tiny speck in the sky. He went back to the place where Daphne had taken root.

"Dear maiden, you are lost to me for all times," he whispered, mourning the loss of yet another love that remained unfulfilled. "But you will be my tree. Your leaves will rest on my victors' brows. You will be there for my triumphs, and for as long as my name exists in this world, so shall yours."

The tree swayed from side to side as though giving a happy consent to the words that Apollo had spoken.

EPILOGUE

"I TOLD YOU, HER CORD WOULD NEVER BE CUT," CLOTHO said to Atropos with a tiny grin on her face.

The three sisters turned and gazed at the dark green cord that had remained untouched for numerous centuries.

"There are a few cords in that corner of our home that have yet to be cut," Atropos admitted.

"Do you think the gods have learned their lesson?" Lachesis lifted a brow.

Clotho laughed. Her laughter echoed throughout the cave and made the numerous cords vibrate and hum softly. "No, of course not. Only the mortals have the capacity to learn from their mistakes. Gods make the same mistakes over and over again because they have nothing to lose. Nothing to learn. They just are. Just as the three of us know nothing except how to spin, measure, and cut."

Atropos and Lachesis nodded knowing the wisdom their youngest sister had just spoken.

Clotho stood up, leaving her seat in front of her spinning wheel for the first time in many years and walked towards Daphne's cord. She hadn't touched it in so long, she often wondered if she had only imagined herself spinning it into existence, yet there it was, a seemingly ordinary hunter green cord. But Clotho could see the silver aura that emanated from the wool. She gently reached out and touched the cord, afraid it would snap in half, but regardless of her fear she gently grazed it.

"No one will ever touch you, beautiful Daphne," she whispered. She sighed and went back to her stool and spun yet another cord into being.

"Whose cord are you spinning this time?" Atropos cut a white cord.

Clotho smiled. "This boy will try to touch the sun wearing borrowed wings. Shall I tell you his story?"